The Julie Avery
Mystery Trilogy

Part 1 - Her New Book

The Julie Avery Mystery Trilogy
Copyright © 2022 by Beverly J. Graves

Published in the United States of America

ISBN   Paperback: 978-1-958030-35-6
ISBN   eBook: 978-1-958030-36-3

All rights reserved. No part of this publication may be reproduced, stored in a retrieval system or transmitted in any way by any means, electronic, mechanical, photocopy, recording or otherwise without the prior permission of the author except as provided by USA copyright law.

The opinions expressed by the author are not necessarily those of ReadersMagnet, LLC. ReadersMagnet, LLC

10620 Treena Street, Suite 230 | San Diego, California, 92131 USA
1.619. 354. 2643 | www.readersmagnet.com

Book design copyright © 2022 by ReadersMagnet, LLC. All rights reserved.

Cover design by Ericka Obando
Interior design by Daniel C. Lopez

The Julie Avery
Mystery Trilogy
Part 1 - Her New Book

Beverly J. Graves

CHAPTER 1

The sound of the roaring wind and raging rain beating against the windows made Julie Avery cringe as she sat down at her desk. Ok, she said to herself, it's that old cliché, *a dark and stormy night*, but not the right kind of atmosphere for a romance novelist! A flash of lightning and the crack of thunder that followed startled her again as she opened her laptop. Maybe this wasn't such a good time to begin her new book. She had promised Richard Beasley, her publishing agent, that she was working on her new book. She hadn't told him she was yet to "put pen to paper" so to speak. The ideas came to her quickly sometimes, but she just couldn't seem to get started now.

The storm had awakened her at 2:22 am and she couldn't go back to sleep. She laid there listening to the storm and thought about how her mother had always been afraid of storms in the night. Julie missed her mom and thought about how proud she had been when Julie had published her first children's book. A nagging reminder drifted through her mind; she must get started writing her new book. In the foggy reaches, a story was forming and she knew that she must gather the thoughts together and put them down quickly before they began to fade.

She had always enjoyed writing late at night or early in the morning when the house was peaceful and ideas drifted in and out. She could type out several pages when the thoughts were coming swiftly; sometimes they came even faster than she could get them on the page. She never understood how writers of long ago did it by pen and paper; not only could she not write quick enough, but if she had, any future typist would never be able to read it!

Why she had the urgent need to write just now in the middle of a thunderstorm in the middle of the night was unsettling. Most novelists, either write a little each day or write when ideas pop into their heads. Julie usually preferred to write a little each day. She had always wanted to be a romance novelist and the stories seemed to come to her easily whenever she sat at her desk. The open laptop often called to her with visions of a warm summer evening and a handsome young man walking in the park holding the hand of a lovely lady with long flowing red hair. Or the picture of the beach on a sunny afternoon, the happy couple running down the sand together and plunging into the waves as they laughed and fell into the crystal blue water. Yes, she knew, clichés again, but there can always be that little twist which makes it unique and Julie loved creating the twists of the story.

Tonight was different though, this feeling of being drawn to her desk was something she had not experienced before. When the storm had made her sit up in bed, she looked at the clock on her bedside stand. The blue glow lit up 2:22 am when she pushed the button on top. That number seemed familiar as she shook the sleep out of her head and put her feet into the pink fuzzy slippers next to her bed. Oh, of course, the date of my birth! Isn't it odd to wake up at that time? The sound of the wind had made her shiver and she reached for her flannel robe draped over the burgundy Queen Anne chair at the foot of the bed. It was early spring and the days had been sunny and warm until the sun went down and the temperature dropped. With tonight's storm the house was even colder. She thought about turning the furnace back on but she decided to stick with her policy of April 1st being the last day of heat she had to pay for. It wouldn't be long before the heat of summer would require the AC. Struggling writers needed to be conservative, she reminded herself as she pulled the soft snuggly robe around her and tightened the belt. She headed to the kitchen to turn on the tea kettle. A hot cup of tea was what she needed. Her cat, Spot, was at the foot of the bed and Julie rubbed his ears as she got up. Spot looked at her with sleepy eyes as if to say 'what are you doing up at this time of night?' He didn't usually sleep on the bed, content to be in his basket by her side, but obviously the storm had woken him too. He followed her into the kitchen and let out a loud meow at being disturbed from the warmth of the bed near Julie. "It's alright, Spot." Julie picked him up and crooned to him as she nuzzled his neck. She had gotten him as a kitten at the pound when she bought the cottage. She didn't want a dog; they required too much attention; walking and grooming. Cats took care of themselves as long as you left out food and water and changed the litter box. His name was *Midnight* the shelter said, but Julie renamed him *Spot*. Silly, of course, since he didn't have any spots on his coal black body. But Julie had been a **Star Trek** fan ever since she had watched an old rerun and fell in love with Data, the human-like android who named his striped cat Spot.

She dropped Spot to the floor when another flash of lightning made a silhouette on the trees outside the kitchen window. Spot let out a little meow at having his snuggling interrupted. Had she seen a figure on the patio? No, she was just being silly, her mind was playing tricks on her. The trees were whipping in the wind and the branches just looked like someone was out there. The storm was making her imagination run wild. Even as a kid, her mother had said, "Julie, your imagination will either get you in trouble one of these days or make you a million dollars". So far she had avoided the trouble, but still hoped for the million dollars.

Her first book had done quite well in the local market but hadn't really reached the national level to warrant fame and fortune. She had some success with her children's books and a couple of short romance stories, but she wanted to write a novel that would indeed make the fortune her mother had predicted. At age thirty-four Julie wasn't sure it would ever happen. She had wanted to be a writer for as long as she could remember. She had gotten good grades in High School and her English teacher had suggested she consider writing. Even in College her Literature professor had encouraged her to pursue writing as a career. So she had majored in Journalism and decided on a career of being a reporter writing her exciting stories about events in far off places. When that hadn't worked out, she returned to writing romance novels but, after endless rejection letters, she had almost given up.

Brandon Jenkins, her best friend in High School had gone into the publishing business after getting his Journalism decree in college and he offered to show a few of her short stories to his boss, Richard Beasley. That had been the start of her somewhat lucrative career. Richard had published several of her short stories while she worked on her first full romance novel. Julie had loved writing it, a love story set during WWII, and she felt quite pleased with it. Richard also had been optimistic about it and Brandon had seen it through the publishing process. He had been excited to deliver the first check for her efforts. Now he and Richard were anxiously awaiting this new book. Brandon had assured Julie that her new book would cement her career in the romance novel business. She just needed to get started on it!

The shrillness of the teakettle's whistle sang out loud between the thunder and flashes of lightning. Julie filled Spot's water bowl and put a few kibble snacks on the floor. It wasn't time to feed him for the day yet, but a little snack wouldn't hurt. She then turned her thoughts to fixing that steaming cup of tea with sugar and cream like she had grown up drinking when she was a child. She still preferred the English way of tea preparation like her mother. Hot, sweet and creamy. Although she could manage it without the cream if necessary, but the sugar was a must. And it had to be hot! If you could put your finger in it, then it wasn't hot enough. Waitresses always looked at her a little annoyed when she sent it back to have them nuke it more. And they really looked at her strangely when she requested coffee creamer with her hot tea order. She sometimes wanted to skip asking to avoid the looks, but the taste of cream and sugar in a cup of very hot Earl Grey was the perfect finishing touch to any meal. And no need to bring her the divided box of Herbal teas to select from, just a bag of Earl Grey suited her fine. Ok, a bag of Lipton would do if they didn't have Earl Grey but please, no caramel apple or wild blueberry flavor. Just the thought of those made her cringe. She would treat herself to a steeping a pot of real loose tea if she was going to be up for the rest of the night. Even in England most everyone had gone to using tea bags, but the fun of mashing a pot of loose tea and using a strainer to pour into your cup brought back lovely childhood memories.

Her Grandmother used to make sure just enough loose tea leaves remained in the bottom of the cup so she could "read" the tea leaves. Oh, what a production she had made of it! She would swill the cup three times around. It had to be three, of course, no more, no less. She would turn the cup upside down in the saucer and then torture her *audience* by making them wait painfully while she *connected* with the spirits. The waiting seemed endless and no amount of antsy squirming on Julie's or her younger sister's part would ever make Grandma budge. The time had to be right. When their patience was near its end, she would lift the cup and then carefully peer into the cup and with pursed lips she would shake her head and say, "Oh, no I mustn't tell you. No, No," adding to the suspense and expectation. What? What? Something bad? A little prodding and pleading would finally get her to reveal a bit of the treasured information the cup was holding. "Do you know anyone with the initial B"? she would ask seriously. Sometimes it was a D or an H. Of course, no matter what letter of the alphabet she chose, they could always think of someone, a friend or family member from which she could weave her tale. Then she would softly begin the story in a voice so low they could barely hear her without leaning in.

Perhaps she saw a boat or a bird flying near the top of the cup. They could be going on a long trip or the bird was bringing news, which could be good or bad depending on her mood at the time. Many times after giving a few good fortunes of meeting someone tall and handsome, marrying with three children, or coming into money very soon, she would end with, "Oh, dear, no, I can't go any further. That's enough." It was as if she couldn't go on; it either was too awful of news to share or it was too tiring interpreting the spiritual messages in the tea leaves. In either case, no amount of pleading would make her continue at this point. The fortune telling was over. You just had to imagine what horrible thing or good fortune she had "seen" in the tea leaves and wait until another day when she could be convinced to share a bit of her otherworldly abilities. Having a British family had always been a special joy and Julie treasured all things connected to her English birthright.

When the pot of tea had steeped to perfection, Julie lifted the tea cozy her grandmother had knitted long ago. It was a bit ragged around the edges, but Julie loved the soft green color with the little pompom on top. You could almost wear it for a hat! She remembered the day her grandmother had given it to her; it was one of those special memories, tea cozy knitted just for her. Julie poured herself a cup and added the sugar and cream, while the storm continued to rage outside her window. She took her hot cup of tea and a biscuit to nibble on and headed down the hall to her office. Spot followed at her feet. She picked him up and snuggled her face into his fur once more as she sat down at her desk with her Earl Grey in the office of the little cottage on the cul-de-sac at the end of the long tree lined lane. She had loved the cottage the moment she saw it. It reminded her of her auntie's cottage in Tilton-on-the-Hill just outside of Leicester, England. The family actually referred to it as a bungalow, but cottage was what always came to Julie's mind when she looked at her own home. The driveway curved in front of the charming white cottage with the blue shutters, so she could enter and exit from either side of the drive. The area was large enough to accommodate an extra vehicle or two for visitors if Julie parked her own car in the attached one-car garage on the left. The kitchen was at the front of the house with the living room behind. The two bedrooms and bath were down the hall at the back of the cottage. A large window box full of flowers overflowed from the window below the sink area. The perfect place to wash dishes and watch the neighborhood up the road. It was what made the decision to purchase instantly; the lovely little English cottage simply had to be hers!

She had decided her office would be in the far back bedroom overlooking the wooded area that sloped downward to fields of yellow rapeseed that were planted for cooking oil and bird feed. On a clear day Julie could see through the trees at the bits of yellow peeking through. The office was actually what would have been the master bedroom ensuite, but Julie knew the large picture window was the exact place she wanted her desk when she had first looked at the cottage with the realtor. The rest of the cottage had one more bedroom and a small bath in the hall, but with the conservatory attached to the back of the garage, it did seem much larger. Julie loved flowers and the wide ledges of the conservatory windows were lined with pots of geraniums of every color. Julie knew she wasn't much of a gardener so the pots of flowers were her respite. She hoped to plant a real English garden someday. That is, *when* she could afford a gardener to take care of it, otherwise it might not survive her non-green thumb.

It would be lovely to have some fresh vegetables amidst the beds of cultivated plants and blossoms.

She sipped her hot cup of Earl Grey as she stared out at the wooded area. The rain still plummeted the woods and it was so dark that she could only see shadows when the lightning flashed. The tea and Spot's contented purring calmed her nerves a bit. She had almost opted for a teabag tonight so she could get to it quicker. But she had decided to wait for the full pot of loose leaves to steep and she was glad she did. The tea was strong and it warmed her inside and out and in spite of the weather raging beyond the window, she felt relaxed as she sat down and opened a new document on the laptop.

Her office was sparsely furnished and cozy, just the way she liked it. No need for a big fancy desk and other paraphernalia. The laptop fit perfectly on her small desk in front of the large window next to the file cabinet where her wireless printer sat. A comfortable desk chair and the necessary office supplies were all she needed. A burgundy loveseat that opened to make a twin sized bed and a small end table with a lamp, completed the furnishings, in case she ever had an overnight guest. The big room could have felt a little cold except for the paintings from her dear friend, Norman Sims, that lined the light beige walls. She loved how he recreated the little villages, churches and English countryside in his watercolors. She felt a great comfort surrounded by his art. The painting of the driveway approaching Stonelodge Farm near Leicester, England and the hillside where the "Old John" lookout tower rose above Bradgate Park at Newtown Linford were her favorites and gave her a peaceful yet sad feeling for her English heritage and a longing to be there. Norman had been such an important part of her life that she felt as if he was an uncle rather than just a family friend. His death just six weeks before her mom passed left an even bigger hole in her heart, but having his paintings near her helped fill the void. They brought back sweet memories of him and her mom and their friendship which could have progressed to love if they had only let it flourish. She chuckled to herself remembering how she had lovingly called him Papa Norman.

Her many trips to visit her British relatives had always been a special part of growing up. Getting to know her Grandmother and Granddad Parnell was an opportunity she had never really appreciated when she was young, but now she wished she could spend more time exploring that heritage. Having Norman's paintings gave her a daily reminder. Perhaps if her next book did well as Richard and Brandon seemed to think, she could afford to go for an extended visit. Maybe rent a real English cottage and live the English country life she longed for.

She was typing the first line of the new book when another flash of lighting showed the same silhouette she thought she had seen in the kitchen. She was certain now; there was someone out there! Living alone in her small cottage at the end of the long lane at the edge of town was a good location for a writer to have peace and quiet, but on a night like this seeing a figure outside was not relaxing! Julie knew she was not imagining it. She was sure it was the same figure as before and she felt a frightened chill run through her body. She looked around the office for something she could use as a weapon if it came to that.

She was reaching for her cell phone when the sound of the doorbell ringing nearly made her jump out of her skin! The goosebumps came up on her arms and the hair on the back of her neck literally felt like it was standing up! Spot had sat up in his basket beside her desk when he heard the doorbell. Julie wondered who could be there at this time of night? She didn't even want to respond to the door but she knew that whoever it was could see that she was awake since the lights were on in the kitchen and the office. She looked at her cell phone as she gingerly walked up the hallway; there were no bars. The bell rang again; someone was definitely out there and wanted her attention! Why would anyone be out at this time of night in this storm? Julie didn't know what to expect. Seeing her umbrella stand near the door she pulled out one with a long handle. The top had a spikey point that she felt would make a good hole in someone if she lunged at them. She didn't know exactly how she could do it, but she felt she needed to be prepared and the feel of it in her hand gave her some semblance of confidence.

She tried to peer through the peephole in the door to see who was there but the rain had fogged over the glass and all she could see was a shadowy figure on her front porch. "Who is it", she called out in the strongest voice she could muster. There was no answer and Julie's grip on the umbrella handle tightened. "I've got a gun in here so you'd best be on your way", she shouted hoping her voice sounded menacing.

"Miss Avery, it's me, Eric Players, your neighbor up the road. I know you don't know me very well, but the power is out at my place and I can't get any cell phone bars. Can you? I need to call for help. It's my dad. I saw your lights were on. Everyone else up the road is dark."

Julie knew that Eric Players did indeed live up the road and that he took care of his ailing father. They had moved in early last Fall and she remembered his dad had been brought into the house on a gurney. She relaxed her grip on the umbrella. The imprint of the handle showed on her fingers as she released it and there were little red marks on the palm of her hand where she had dug in her fingernails. Cautiously she opened the door the length of the security chain and peered around it. Eric Players stood there dripping wet with a look of alarm on his face. "Oh, thank God, I saw your light. Can I come in and use your phone; I don't have any bars, do you? My dad has oxygen and a feeding tube along with an IV drip that all operate with electricity and with the power out…." His voice trailed off in exasperation.

Julie wasn't sure she wanted to open the door and let a stranger in at this time of night but she certainly could try 911. "Oh, dear, sure, I can call 911 for you if my landline is working; I don't have any bars on my cell either; the storm has taken it out. I just hope an ambulance can get here in this storm."

"He's alright for now, I don't think I need 911 or an ambulance, but I need to call the hospital with a question about the equipment. I thought those things had a battery backup but it doesn't seem to be working either. I can probably fix it with a couple of instructions. I won't be long, a quick call and I will hurry back to dad; I don't like leaving him alone for long."

Julie was still hesitant, but she said, "Alright, let me close the door and remove the chain. I can see if my land line is still working. The storm may have taken it out too. My mother insisted I keep it for emergencies. She didn't trust cell phones, so I guess she was right." Julie opened the door and stepped back.

Eric entered and turned to her in apology, "I'm so sorry, to come here at this hour and to drip all over your floor, but I need to find out what to do for dad."

"No problem", Julie said. "The phone is in my office. This way." She led the way down the narrow hallway to the back of the cottage. Spot tagged along beside her letting out a loud meow. He wasn't used to having a stranger in the house and he voiced his opinion. "I hope I didn't scare you or your cat," Eric said. "I knocked on the door first. I didn't see the doorbell button until later when the lightning flashed again. I went around back to where I saw your light and I was going to knock on the window, but decided not to. I knew it would scare you for sure."

"Yes, thank you for that. The storm was unnerving enough and I did think I saw someone outside. Living here alone at the end of the cul-de-sac can be a little disturbing during a thunderstorm like this. I'm not usually up at this time of night, but that loud crack of thunder woke me and then I had an idea come into my head for my new book so I decided to sit down and write a few paragraphs. Here's the phone. Do you need the directory?" Julie felt like she was spilling out information nervously and she tried to calm herself as she handed him the phone. A man at her door in the middle of the night was unsettling her and she took a deep breath to stop herself from blurting out anything further. *Living here alone, what on earth made me say that?'* She chided herself. Her mother was probably flipping over in her grave!

"No, I have a number to call for emergencies. Thank you." Eric smiled at her and she felt herself relax a bit.

Julie walked out into the hall to give Eric some privacy for his call. When he finished, he joined her. "They said it does have a backup battery but sometimes it takes a few minutes to kick in when the pump loses power. I guess I just got panicky when the power went out and the lights on the machine went dark. Dad was sleeping peacefully but I still got worried. I just ran out when I saw your lights were still on. The whole neighborhood is out; how do you still have power?"

"Oh, I have a backup generator. You know, writers don't want to lose their creations in a storm. It was my mom's idea. I guess she was right again." Julie laughed nervously still feeling stupid.

"Good idea, I understand perfectly. And it certainly was a Godsend for me tonight. I didn't know you were a writer. Lucky for me that you write at night during a thunderstorm."

Julie could see that he was teasing her and it made her a bit more comfortable. "I'm glad I could help. How is your dad? I saw an ambulance brought him to the house when you first moved here last Fall." Julie asked. "What's wrong with him?"

"Cancer". Eric answered quickly. He's stable for now and but we don't know how long he may have. I'm no nurse but I hope I can take care of him until the end. He's been a good father and it's the least I can do."

"It must be hard. I'll say a prayer for you and your dad." Julie felt a bit awkward as she pulled her robe tighter around her and started to lead Eric up the hallway. She wanted to get him out of the house before she said any other dumb thing about living alone. She felt stupid enough still holding the umbrella *weapon* in her hand.

"Thank you. You've already been an angel in disguise. I'm so glad the storm woke you up. It really was lucky for me, I guess, that writers work from home at all hours of the day or night.

Thanks again. I hope I didn't make too much of a mess on your floors. Sorry, thanks." And with that, Eric hurried out the door into the teeming rain and disappeared quickly into the darkness as he made his way back up the road to his house. Julie looked at the floor and saw the wet footsteps leading from the front door, down the hall, and into her office. No more sleeping tonight, she thought as she went to get the mop from the kitchen pantry.

By the time she had cleaned the mess on the floor, her tea had gotten cold so she went to the kitchen to reheat it in the microwave. 'What a night! I should be writing a mystery suspense novel instead of a romance story,' she mused. As she headed down the hallway, Spot followed and curled up in his basket again, content that things were back as they should be. Julie sat down in front of the laptop with her refreshed hot cup of tea; she suddenly realized that the inspiration she had had earlier was gone. She stared at the blank screen for a few minutes as she drank her tea and wondered about Eric Players and his dad. She hoped that everything was alright with them. She made a mental note to check with him in the morning when his power was back on and their cell service was restored. The neighborhood association regularly sent around names and phone numbers whenever someone new moved into the area so if she could find that memo, she would give him a call.

She silently thanked her mother for suggesting that she install a backup generator. Julie hadn't thought it was necessary at the time, but Mom had insisted that losing power and losing several chapters of a book in progress would not be fun. With that somewhat misguided logic in mind, Julie had agreed and purchased the generator. Tonight she was glad she had.

She closed her eyes and her mind drifted to Eric Players standing in her doorway. Even dripping wet he was not hard to look at, she thought to herself. He was tall, maybe 6'2" Julie guessed. At 5'9" Julie liked a tall man. The rain had soaked his T-shirt and jacket, so she could see the muscles in his arms and chest. She wondered if he worked out, surely he must. His brown hair looked thick and maybe just a little long for her tastes, but, any man who would take on caring for a dying parent, must be a good guy she decided. She wondered why they had not crossed paths more often. She remembered when he had moved in last Fall, the neighborhood ladies organized a backyard BBQ to welcome him. She had attended but didn't give much notice of him at the time since all the other ladies were busy being gaga over him, shades of **Desperate Housewives**! Julie had decided that she didn't want to be part of the *new guy on the block* club.

He had kept to himself over the past several months and Julie surmised it was because of his dad's illness. She wondered why there was no other family. Where were the wife and kids? She hadn't seen anyone else leaving the house. Maybe she would learn a bit more when she called him later. She finished her tea and thought, 'well, now that writing is out of the question, best to head back to bed for at least a couple of hours sleep. I hope that strong Earl Grey won't keep me awake.'

It did prove to be a restless, useless night. Julie couldn't sleep or write. Early the next morning, when she was at the kitchen counter having her morning oatmeal with grape jam like her British granddad, her desk phone rang. She hesitated to answer; 'not a robo call or a scammer this early in the morning on my land line!' But her writer's curiosity got the best of her so she hurried down the hall to her office, picked up the receiver, and said "Hello?"

"Julie, Eric Players. I hope you don't mind I jotted down your phone number last night. I wanted to call and thank you again for your generosity. I'm sure it was a bit scary to have a stranger at your door during that storm last night, especially when I had been prowling around the yard. I apologize. That was silly of me. I was just so concerned for my dad, I wasn't thinking."

"Oh, don't worry about it. I had my trusty umbrella ready to smash any intruder."

"I thought you said you had a gun? That put a bit of fear in me."

"Sorry", Julie laughed. "I was trying to be brave and sound menacing."

"You had me convinced."

"I guess my mom taught me how to defend myself and after all, I am a writer with a vivid imagination."

"And a good one apparently. Your mom's idea about the generator was good too. The whole neighborhood was dark. That's why I came to your place."

"Yep, backup generator saves the day or night. You know us writers, don't want to lose our hard work in a power outage. My mom was always right." Julie felt like she was rambling on like a school girl. Eric Players had sparked something.

"Smart. I should look into that so I won't have to lurk out into the dark rainy night for help when the next storm comes along."

"Oh, now you sound like a mystery writer. If I need any tips, I'll call you. How is your Dad doing? I was going to call you today and ask, but you beat me to the punch. Besides, I couldn't find your cell phone number, silly me."

"He's none the worse for wear. He slept through it all. I wanted to tell him about my midnight walk in the rain though. He would have gotten a chuckle out of it. Especially if I told him the pretty lady down the road threatened me with a gun."

Julie laughed. "I'm so sorry."

"No, you were right to be cautious and prepared. Thanks to your mom, you made me a believer."

"Is there anything I can do to help? It must be hard taking care of your dad and working too."Julie hoped he would share a bit more information about himself and any possible family, even though she knew she hadn't seen anyone else come and go from the house. But then, she hadn't really taken time to look that often. When she was writing she was at the back of the cottage in her office where the window looked out over the wooded area. It was pretty but remote. It was the way she preferred it most of the time, but she was a bit sorry she hadn't gotten to know her neighbors better.

"Thank you for the offer, but I think I have it all under control as long as the power doesn't go out. Thanks again, Julie." And with that he was gone.

Julie hoped she hadn't offended him by offering to help. He had finished the conversation so abruptly and hung up. She hadn't meant to pry. But she was curious as to why such an attractive man wasn't married with a family and why he had moved to their small town of Monique, IN with his terminally ill father. The writer in her began imaging all sorts of possible explanations. 'Was he on the run from the law? No, he was hiding from his two ex-wives hoping they wouldn't find him! Alimony and child support was no joke with two wives, not to mention any possible bigamy charges. Nah, that storyline was as old as the hills'. Julie knew there was a simple feasible answer and eventually she would find out.

Right now, she needed to write. Not her new book, but her grocery list. After last night's storm she knew she should stock the cupboards better. She wasn't much of a cook, but having bread, milk, cereal, some hamburger and canned goods and of course, tea, on hand was a must if the power went out again for any length of time. Oh, and cat food. Spot would never forgive her if she forgot that! She felt confident in her generator, but you never know. Being prepared was best. Somewhere in her pantry was a small BBQ grill, so she should get some charcoal briquettes.

Grocery list in hand, Julie backed her 2014 Chevy Sonic out of the garage and drove around the cul-de-sac towards town. The little car was the perfect fit for her. It handled nicely and was easy to park and she loved the shiny red color. She had always named her cars and when she had bought this one new, Red Hot was the color of the paint, so Red Hot Mama was the only name that worked!

The grocery store wasn't far and Red Hot Mama had her there in no time. The supermarket was part of a small strip mall, of sorts, about ten blocks from Julie's cottage. She would have walked or rode her bike on a nice day like this, but with a lot of groceries to carry, Red Hot Mama was the best choice. She would get the bike out later now that the weather was clearing up and it was getting a little warmer. She enjoyed the rides, but only if the weather was accommodating. She didn't relish riding in the rain even if it was a summer shower. She had made that mistake last June and even though it was warm enough, the rain hitting her in the face as she pedaled her way home was not fun. She vowed to check the weather report before taking another long bike ride.

The mall parking lot looked busy and Julie hoped the store wouldn't be. She vehemently hated grocery shopping and only did it when absolutely necessary. Julie glanced at the mall; there was a Chinese restaurant, a small book store, a shoe store and one of those thrift places at the end of the row of buildings had a sign that read "Clearing out bargains". Julie had gotten several great deals there. Her mom had taught her how to be frugal and heaven knows a struggling writer had to be! She made a mental note to stop in there again soon and see what was on the racks. Perhaps their sign was the explanation for the busy parking lot. Monique shoppers always liked a good bargain. Her attention turned to the supermarket. 'Let's get this over with.' She sighed and took a deep breath. As she entered and got her cart, she looked around and saw that there weren't too many people at the checkout lanes. She breathed a sigh of relief and her stomach settled down a bit. So silly to feel this way about grocery shopping, but she couldn't do much about it, it happened every time.

A few minutes later her cart was full, practically to over flowing and she was glad that she had found everything quickly even though she hadn't realized she needed so many things. But once she had headed down the aisle, she saw she was indeed low on many items she hadn't thought about and the cart had filled up in no time. Running out of toilet paper would be a disaster so she knew she should stock up on that as well. The big bundle sat precariously on top of the full cart. She headed for the checkout lanes and as she turned the corner she bumped into another cart coming from the opposite direction. She had been looking down at her list and didn't see it turning the corner into her aisle. The big bundle of toilet paper slid off the top and bounced to the floor. "Oh, crap," Julie said out loud. When she looked up, she saw the smiling face of Eric Players!

CHAPTER 2

Eric Players was an architect, well, at least he had been. And a good one, he had won the AIA twice and had been nominated for the prestigious Pritzker Prize. The Pritzker Prize *"honors a living architect whose built work demonstrates a combination of those qualities of talent, vision, and commitment, which has produced consistent and significant contributions to humanity and the built environment through the art of architecture."*

He had hoped that he would be nominated again for his current project until the accident at the construction site ended his career. The same accident that injured his dad who had been the crew boss for the construction company.

Yes, he had told Julie that his dad had cancer, but that was a necessary lie. No one in Monique needed to know the details of the accident and why they had moved here. Everyone believed it to be an accident at first, but then since Eric was the architect, he ended up taking the responsibility to avoid a costly lawsuit. The construction company refused any notion of accepting blame and demanded a statement of guilt which meant Eric's architectural firm would be held in jeopardy. Eric had tried to explain to his bosses the problem was not in his design but in the inadequate equipment, materials and safety procedures of Streeter Construction who had been hired for the job. Too many overages and extended work orders had come across his desk and Eric had started to look into things.

When the crack had developed in the floor of the tenth floor, Eric had questioned his dad about the quality of the cement and rebar. Ben Players had immediately arched his back, crossed his arms, glared at his son and claimed there was nothing to be concerned about. When Eric pursued the issue, they had ended up in an argument over who was right. Ben Players defended his boss as diligently as Eric defended his and the two men became estranged. So without any concrete (*pardon the pun*) proof of their negligence and use of inferior products, after months of meetings with the lawyers, Eric could do nothing but sign the papers admitting that his design was flawed. If he hadn't, Folder Architecture and Streeter Construction would have both gone under. Fred Streeter and George Folder had agreed to no further lawsuits and the lawyers kept the accident details and the settlement information out of the newspapers. Folder and Streeter shared the cost of the rebuilding of the project using another architect as the lead contact with the new contractor. Do to the low publicity, as far as the general public was concerned, it had been an unfortunate accident. The two CEO's also agreed to share the cost of the settlement with the insurance companies for the injured and families of the deceased. It was a huge expense for both companies but at least they could remain in business as long as there were no further lawsuits. Other than the initial news report when the building collapsed, that was it, and the rebuild continued without Eric and Ben. The lawyers had done their job of sweeping the entire thing under the rug along with Eric and his dad as two of the casualties.

Eric felt certain that his dad was aware of the underhanded operations at Streeter Construction and Eric had fully intended to find the proof he needed to confront his dad and bring it all out in open. But, then, the crack in the cement of the tenth floor gave way and the entire structure began to crumble. Ben had been on the sixth floor at the time of the accident and had tumbled into the chasm that opened up as it split apart taking him and other workers with it. He had suffered multiple injuries, broken bones, crushed ribs and a severe head injury. In addition, inhaling cement dust as the building came down, damaged his lungs. It was a hard fall for a 63-year-old.

Several of the younger workers were injured as well and two had died at the scene. Streeter Construction immediately placed the blame on Folder Architecture and the lawyers began the endless meetings as to who was at fault. Months of depositions delayed the project and the investors in the Capitol Avenue Apartments began pushing for a settlement. It was only with Folder Architecture finally agreeing to sign a statement admitting a flaw in Eric's structural design being the cause that kept Streeter and Folder in operation and everyone out of court. The lawyers worked out the details with all the parties, but, Eric, of course, lost his job and his license. His bosses were sorry, but his termination was part of the settlement agreement. That could have been the end of that story, but Eric was pissed and he wanted more answers. He vowed he would get them no matter what the cost.

Life went on for most everyone, except for Eric and Ben, their lives after the accident were not to be the same. Eric soon found that getting another job as an architect was out of the question without his license and no firm would even consider hiring him, even as a consultant. Financially, he wasn't worried; he had made good money over the past several years and invested it well. He applied for Ben's disability so they could live a modest but comfortable life. His car was paid for, so there were no other expenses other than his dad's care. But he wanted vindication and he was consumed with the thought of it. He knew his dad was the key to information.

Eric hadn't wanted to leave Pennsylvania, but even old friends became distant after the accident. No one said anything, it was just those unanswered questions and silent comments that hung in the air. He could tell each time he ran into a friend or someone from the construction site that they were uncomfortable around him. Everyone had seemed supportive at first, but eventually phone calls went unreturned and conversations seemed to stop immediately if he walked into one of their favorite restaurants or bar. After several weeks he knew there was no point in trying and besides taking care of his dad at home after he left the hospital was taking up a lot of Eric's time. He supposed he could have taken Ben to a facility where he would get professional care, but Eric had his reasons for keeping Ben at home. He felt his dad knew more than he would admit about the accident and Eric wanted to be close if and when more facts came out. Eric wanted his questions answered and he felt his dad had them. Things would never be the same with his friends and his life in general, so moving to a new location and starting over seemed like a good decision.

Monique, Indiana had been a good choice and an easy one to make. Eric had simply taken out a map, closed his eyes and put his finger on it. When he saw Indiana, he thought, 'Ok, where in Indiana?' He got an Indiana road map and did the same. His finger landed on Monique, a small town of 4,235 people. No one there would know about the accident so it was the perfect place. He couldn't bear the thought of going through explanation after explanation. A small town was the answer. When he had looked into housing prices, he had been pleasantly surprised as well. Nothing like Philadelphia. When he had sold his downtown loft apartment and rented out Ben's little house in Middletown, there had been plenty to purchase the beautiful 2,500 sq ft home on the cul-de-sac in Monique with a tidy sum left over. It was a comfortable space with 3 bedrooms, all with ensuite facilities. A well-appointed kitchen with all the modern conveniences and sliding doors leading out to a lovely garden and patio. The family selling the home was very motivated to sell since Mr. Procter's job was moving them across country.

Unfortunately, Mr. Procter had mentioned his extensive flower garden and how the neighbors had admired it. Eric didn't care much for gardening, but he figured he'd better keep it up or it would raise unwanted questions from nosy neighbors, so the first thing he did was hire a man to take care of it for him. All in all, Eric felt like he got a good deal on the house and he had moved his dad into the bedroom down the hall from the master suite.

Across the hall at the end of the hallway was the third bedroom that Eric thought might be used by a live-in caregiver if he felt he needed one in the future. So far he had managed to take care of his dad without any problems. Keeping him sedated had been the best option. Eric hadn't wanted to go through any more arguing with his dad and when the doctor suggested heavy sedation to ease Ben's discomfort, Eric realized it would end the arguments as well. Eric knew his dad was in a lot of pain and arguing with him at the hospital hadn't helped matters so when the doctor said medically induced coma, Eric knew that was the answer. Eric got the necessary equipment, the oxygen pump, a feeding tube, catheter and IV sedation. With some minor instructions Eric was able to manage at home. The sedation kept Ben pain free and the medically induced coma would let his body heal naturally. The doctor couldn't say if Ben would make a complete recovery, but the coma was his best chance for now. Eric knew he probably couldn't keep his dad sedated at home indefinitely. He might have to hire a live-in nurse later when Ben recovered to the point of removing the machines. Right now it was the perfect decision because it would give Eric the opportunity to look into the events leading up to the accident without having to explain his actions daily to his dad or anyone else. Once he knew the truth and had proof, he could explain it all to his dad and to Streeter Construction and to Folder Architecture. So for now Ben would sleep peacefully. It was the best solution. The little scare with the power outage though could have literally been their *wake-up* call, so Eric vowed to get a backup generator like Julie's.

When he thought about the generator, Eric's thoughts again drifted to Julie. After talking to her that morning, he had wanted to see her again. He was a bit sorry he had ended the call so abruptly when she had asked if she could help with his dad in any way. He knew that he shouldn't have lied about his dad's illness. The response of cancer had just seemed easier than a full explanation. Going into detail about the accident and losing his job, his friends and his home just wasn't something he wanted to go into right then. Maybe after he had the answers he needed, he would be able to explain everything. The thought that his dad might have been at fault concerned Eric and he desperately needed to know the details. At this point, he couldn't prove his dad had been involved deliberately in fraud on the jobsite, but he hoped he would find the answers eventually. He just didn't want to talk about it now.

He liked Julie, she was very attractive and seemed like a pleasant person he told himself. She was tall, Eric guessed about 5'8" or 9". She was slim and trim and Eric wondered if she had been an athlete. He had seen her riding her bike past his house on several occasions. Her blonde hair was cut in a soft wavy bob that framed her face and she had the most wonderful blue eyes. No, they were more like a dusty grey/blue, but with a sparkle that he thought he saw in spite of that stormy night they met. When they bumped into each other at the grocery store, they had laughed and he saw that the sparkle in her eyes was definitely there.

"Oh, hi, Eric. Looks like we had the same idea after last night's storm that we shouldn't leave our cupboards so bare." Julie smiled and Eric saw how her whole face lit up.

"That's exactly what I was thinking. Silly of me not to keep things stocked. I don't cook much for myself and dad has a feeding tube, so I don't shop often, but I should keep a few more canned goods and other staples in case of emergency. And I'm checking on an extra battery for dad's pumps. I'm going to look into getting an emergency generator too. I hadn't thought of that, but it sure would have come in handy last night."

"I know I'm glad I have mine." Julie felt a rise in her temperature creeping up the back of her neck. Eric's presence was affecting her more than just a casual bump of their grocery carts.

"Being a caregiver is still new to me. I've been thinking about advertising for a live-in nurse. The house is big enough and there is an extra room available across the hall with its own bathroom." Eric suggested, although he was just making conversation. He really didn't want a live-in nurse poking around and asking questions.

"Oh, that might be a good idea. I'll let you know if I hear of anyone." Julie answered but in her mind she was thinking, 'No, you don't need a woman in the house.'

"Thanks, that's good of you." They stood there in a bit of awkward silence with their shopping carts linked together at the corner of the aisle. Julie backed up and Eric's cart came with hers.

"Oh, geez, look at that. Sorry." Embarrassed, she tried to pull them apart.

"No problem. Let me get them." Eric separated the carts and paused. There wasn't anything else to say right then, so he turned to head to the checkout line. "See you later maybe?"

Julie nodded and watched as he walked away. 'He *is* quite good looking', she thought to herself.

Eric was thinking the same about her as he placed his groceries on the checkout counter. 'Whoa, Eric Players, settle down, you don't need to get involved with anyone right now. You've got plenty on your plate with taking care of dad and investigating the accident. Just leave any thoughts of her alone.'

Groceries paid for and bagged, Eric headed for the parking lot. As he crossed the pavement, he noticed a blonde lady getting into a cute little red car next to his 2018 BMW. 'Nah, couldn't be!! Yep, sure enough.'

Julie looked up after loading her bags in the back seat behind her side of the car and saw Eric approaching with a big grin on his face. "How did you beat me out here? I thought I had a full cart. We seem destined to bump into each other."

"Literally," Julie laughed remembering the entangled carts in the grocery aisle. "The guy at the fast lane waved me over. I guess he wasn't very busy."

Eric thought, 'I'd wave her over too', as he began loading his groceries behind his driver's seat also. When he closed the door he noticed the dented gash in Julie's passenger side. "Hey, what happened to your car?"

"What do you mean?" Julie asked in surprise.

"There's a big *owie* over here."

"What?"

"Yeh, come look. You weren't in an accident recently?"

"No!" Julie exclaimed as she walked around the front of her car. "Oh, you've got to be kidding me!"

"I didn't do it, I swear! Grocery carts are the only thing I've bumped into lately."

"Why didn't you tell me when we were in the store?" Julie was getting upset.

"I didn't know this was your car. I'm sorry. I shouldn't have said anything. You would have noticed it later. But, then again, you probably would have thought I did it and didn't tell you. This is awful."

"Oh, my cute little Red Hot Mama." Tear started to come to Julie's eyes. She did love that car.

"What? Who?" Eric asked with a touch of surprise in his voice. "You named your car?"

"Yes", Julie said indignantly. "I've always named my cars. And Red Hot Mama was my favorite."

"I'm so sorry", Eric commiserated. "But where did you get the name Red Hot Mama?"

"From her color of course". Julie was getting a bit defensive. It was called Red Hot and I added the Mama part."

Eric gave out a hearty laugh even though he was thinking how the name fit her exactly.

"It's not that funny." Julie said feeling her temper rising. She was mad enough about the injury to her car without Eric making fun of her naming it.

"I'm sorry", said Eric trying to get control of himself. "But I was just thinking about the news report. *Red Hot Mama was struck by a hit and run driver in the Monique Mall parking lot today. Police have no clues, but patrons of the Mall will be questioned extensively as the investigation gets underway.* You got to admit it's a bit funny."

"No, I don't have to admit that. I love this car and now look at her."

"Alright, if it will make you feel any better, I'll tell you a secret." Eric leaned in to whisper in Julie's ear. "I name my cars too. This one is White Thunder."

"Oh, yeh, of course you do." Julie managed to grumble as she said it, but inside she started to smile at the thought of Eric naming his cars also.

"You're insured I hope?" Eric asked.

"Of course. I'll call my insurance agent when I get home."

"Uh, none of my business, but shouldn't you call them now? And maybe the police. After all, it was a hit and run. Maybe you should stay here and wait for them to come check out the scene of the crime." Eric gave Julie a wink.

"You're right. I was just so frazzled to see Red Hot Mama like this. Maybe somebody did see it happen." Julie got out her cell phone and dialed the local police station. "I need to report a car accident at the Monique Mall. Someone hit my car in the parking lot... No, no one was injured. I wasn't in it at the time. It was parked and I was in the grocery store... No, I didn't see it happen, I just came out with my groceries and saw it... Ok, I will wait here for an officer to arrive. Thank you."

Julie turned to Eric. "Well, I guess I'll be waiting here." She leaned against the side of her car with an exasperated sigh.

"Do you have any perishables? Milk, meat?" Eric inquired.

"Oh, yes, I do. Damn, what do I do now?" Julie could feel the tears starting to well up. She took a deep breath and held them in. She was embarrassed enough at the situation and having this handsome man see her cry again would be too much.

"I could I take them home with me and put the bag in my refrigerator and you can stop and get them later" Eric suggested.

"Oh, would you really? Yes, that would be great. Thanks." With relief Julie sorted through the bags and put all the perishables into one.

Eric took them and with a smile said, "Don't worry, the police and insurance company will sort things out. I wish I could stay and help, but I probably should get this stuff to the frig." Julie nodded again and watched as he put her bag in his car. As he drove away she realized that not only was he good looking but a really nice guy as well.

It was an hour later before the police were through with their questions and report. In the meantime, Julie called her insurance agent and gave him the details. He said there was no need to worry; her policy would cover the damage. She just needed to get two estimates. Was the car drivable, he had asked? Julie said, she didn't think so, the front wheel base was bent back and rubbing on the frame. The police officer confirmed her assessment and said he would give her a ride home. The tow truck arrived and Red Hot Mama was pulled out of the parking lot.

Julie asked the officer to drop her off at Eric's house so she could get her groceries. She thanked him as she got out and said a silent prayer at living in a small town where people were nice and friendly. Except, of course, for the idiot who had sideswiped her car and not left a note!!

Eric saw her getting out of the police car and opened his front door to greet her. "Come in. I've put the coffee pot on. I thought you might need a cup to calm your nerves."

"That is sweet of you, but I don't drink coffee. I'm half British so tea is my drink of choice. I have a new box in my grocery bag." The realization hit Julie that she had left her groceries in her damaged car. "Oh, crap. They're in my car and it's being towed to the repair shop storage yard. No! I should have stayed in bed this morning."

"Not to worry, Eric's **Uber** driver at your service." He gave a dramatic bow bending at the waist. "I'd be happy to take you there."

Julie laughed. "We seem to be rescuing each other on a regular basis. You are so nice."

"Just let me just check on dad and then we can go." Eric walked down the hall and Julie glanced around the room while she waited. She had only entered the front door and living room area but what she saw was neat and tidy. The décor was mid-century modern and looked a bit worn, but masculine and adequate for a single man. She wondered what Eric did for a living. He seemed to be financially comfortable and since he had to be there for his dad most of the time, she knew he probably didn't go out to work so he must have a job that allowed him to work from home. A question to ask at some later time she decided.

Eric returned from the hallway and said, "Dad is sleeping, of course, like he does all of the time. The sedation in his IV keeps him that way. I do sometimes wish he was more alert, but I don't want him to be in pain, so…" Eric let the sentence trail off and quickly changed the subject. "So, let's go get those groceries. Maybe there's something in those bags for lunch!"

Julie hadn't thought about fixing lunch, but maybe it was a good way to thank Eric and repay him for his kindness. "Well, as long as you are okay with soup and sandwiches, I can do it. I'm not much of a cook. When you live alone, there is no need to prepare big fancy meals. I can do it, but it's usually much easier to have soup and a sandwich at my desk when I'm writing. My mom was a good cook and I did learn to make a great roast with Yorkshire pudding."

"That sounds wonderful. I'm usually a soup and sandwich guy too. I agree, it never seems like it's worth all the trouble of preparing a big meal and sitting down alone to eat it. But,

I do make a mean pot of chili and Spaghetti Bolognese is my specialty." They laughed comfortably as they drove to the car repair shop.

It didn't take long to grab the other bags of groceries and head back to Eric's house. Julie opened a can of beef and barley soup and made two ham sandwiches with cheese. Eric raved about how wonderful lunch was. Julie laughed at him and asked if this was the first time he had eaten beef and barley soup with ham and cheese sandwiches.

"No, but it is the first time I didn't have to make them. And now I'm enjoying them with such pleasant company at the table."

Julie agreed. "You're right, I've enjoyed it more too. I eat a lot of sandwiches at my desk. It's nice to have someone to talk to while I eat."

"We should do it more often. I can impress you with my chili making and you can make more sandwiches."

"Oh, but you said Spaghetti Bolognese was your specialty. If we are going to do this again, I want the specialty of the house," Julie teased.

"Definitely can do." Eric replied. "Shall we make it a date then?"

Julie hesitated at the suggestion of a date. She liked Eric and he certainly was attractive but she wasn't in the market for dating. "That does sound nice, Eric, but I am really busy with my new book. Maybe some other time?"

Eric could see by the look on her face that the conversation was taking a turn for the worse. He hadn't meant to say 'date'. He just enjoyed her company and having another meal with her would have been enjoyable. "I'm sorry, I didn't mean…."

"It's okay. When I've finished the new book then maybe we can think about it. You know how writers are; the work comes before anything else. And I should be getting back to it now." She got up and began clearing their dishes.

"Leave those, I can get them later. I don't have anything else to do right now. Go, I understand."

Julie felt a little uncomfortable. She hoped she hadn't offended him. She didn't mean to do that. "Thanks again for helping me get my groceries. Sorry to run off so soon and I just remembered I didn't feed Spot before I left for the store. I didn't think I would be gone that long."

"Spot? I didn't see a dog at your house."

"Nope, no dog, just the black cat named Spot."

"Funny name for a cat, isn't it? And I didn't see any spots on him."

"Probably, but I'm a Trekkie and I couldn't resist." Julie confessed.

"Trekkie, you don't mean you watch those silly **Star Trek** reruns."

Julie was a little offended, but she thought maybe he was joking. "Of course, don't you? I've loved them since I was a kid."

"Sorry, never watched them. Guess I was too busy working."

"Well, I will introduce you to them sometime, I have a complete DVD collection." Julie picked up her grocery bags and headed for the door.

Eric shook his head in amazement at this attractive lady who watched old **Star Trek** shows. He knew he wanted to get to know her better. "Do you need a ride home?"

"Oh, no, I can manage. It's just down the hill." Julie put a bag in each arm and draped the third one over her left shoulder.

"Will you need a ride anywhere else?" Eric was hoping he could have the chance to see her again soon.

"Well, not that I know of. The insurance company is providing a rental car until Red Hot Mama is repaired or I find another one. They said they would drop it off later today. If she can't be repaired, I'll have to shop for a new car and I hate shopping." Julie dreaded the thought of it. She actually hated all kinds of shopping and rarely went to the mall, except when she really needed something. She much preferred to look through catalogs or shop online. Walking endlessly through department stores did not appeal to her at all. Her mother had the shopper bug and had dragged Julie to store after store when she was young and Julie had learned to hate it.

"Would you like for me to do some checking online for something in the area? If I can find some possibilities, it would save you some time." Eric suggested. He didn't know why he had said that, other than it was an excuse to see her again. He knew he should just leave it alone, but he was drawn to this pretty blonde lady.

Julie didn't want to be indebted to him, but the offer was nice. "Oh, you don't have to do that. You don't have time with taking care of your dad."

"But I do. Dad doesn't require a lot of care. I usually have his bath done early and he sleeps the rest of the time. I'm on the computer anyway, doing some research, so checking out some vehicles wouldn't be a bother at all."

Julie wondered what research he was doing, but didn't feel she should ask. "Well, if you are sure it won't be an inconvenience, I will accept your gracious offer."

"I'll get right on it." Eric smiled.

"Thank you, Eric, you have been a lifesaver today." He really had been a great help and she had enjoyed lunch immensely.

"Just returning the favor after the storm last night." Eric reminded her.

"It seems like we have developed a mutual saver pact." Julie laughed. "Right now I need to get home with these groceries. Again, thanks for your help." She turned and walked out the front door.

"It's my pleasure. It's not often I get to be the knight in shining armor and rescue the damsel in distress." Eric called after her.

"There you go again, trying to be a writer. You will, of course, need to get away from those old clichés. I'll talk to you later." As Julie headed down the hill to her cottage, she tried to give a little wave. The grocery bags were heavy and she thought maybe she should have taken Eric's offer to drive her home. But that would have been silly. 'Buckle up there, girl, you can manage,' she told herself.

Eric watched as she walked away and noticed she was struggling a bit with the bags. He wanted to hurry out and help her carry them, but he gave it a second thought. He had offered. If she wanted his help, she would have agreed. Best to leave it at that. He headed to his computer and decided to start looking for cars for sale in the area.

CHAPTER 3

Several days later as Julie was sitting at her computer, she found herself staring out the window into the woods remembering the stormy night the past week when she had seen a shadowy figure out there who turned out to be her neighbor in need of help. She smiled to herself thinking about Eric that night and then the following morning when they literally ran into each other at the grocery store; well, their carts did. And how Eric helped her after she discovered her car had been damaged in the parking lot. It all seemed like a strange funny dream. They had returned from the car repair storage lot with her groceries and she had come into his kitchen and fixed beef barley soup and ham and cheese sandwiches for lunch. How bizarre! It was like they were old friends.

Soup and sandwich had been her favorite cheering up kind of lunch when she was a kid. Her mom had always known what to do whenever Julie was down. She just had a knack for seeing Julie troubled over something and fixing hot soup and sandwich just when Julie needed them the most. Oh, how she wished those days were still here. It had been twelve years since her mom had died and Julie missed her more now than she had then. In her later years, Julie realized that her mom had been right about a lot of things. She valued her mother's opinion and wished she could talk to her now.

'Mom', Julie thought. 'What do I do? I find myself interested in a man I barely know. But we seem to enjoy each other's company and it's so easy. You know how I've always felt awkward about meeting people and how backward I can be around them. But Eric is different. He makes me feel comfortable, even when he was a dripping wet stranger at my door at 2:22 in the morning. Isn't that funny, mom, me waking up at the time of my birthdate? What do you suppose that means?'

Julie shook herself out of the daydream and stared at the pages of her new book. She hadn't written much yet. Her mind kept drifting away. There was a story there she was sure, but it just wasn't quite ready to flow from her brain to her fingers. The phone rang just then and she looked at the display and recognized the number. It was Kevin, her insurance agent. "Hi Kevin. What's the good news?"

"Well, Julie, not such good news. The adjuster said it's totaled." Kevin said apologetically.

"What? How can that be? It was only the passenger door." Julie was shocked to think that Red Hot Mama would be a total loss.

"Nope, remember the front wheel was bent back into the frame? It was not drivable, you know. Well, that's pretty expensive to fix and more than the car is worth, I'm afraid. We can total it out and get you a check by next week. In the meantime, you can start looking for a new car." Kevin offered cheerfully.

"Yes, I know I will have to, but I really want Red Hot Mama back."

Kevin laughed. "Red Hot Mama?"

"I know, I know, it's crazy, but I have always named my cars and that little red Sonic was special. I hope I can find another one just like it."

"Well, good luck with the shopping." Kevin said with a smile in his voice. "Your check will be in the mail in a couple days. Bye, Julie, sorry about Red Hot Mama."

"Thanks, Kevin." Julie was glad she had such good insurance and such a pleasant agent, but that phone call just made Julie more depressed. She wanted her real mama. She would have comforted her. But Julie knew she would have to settle for a cup of hot Earl Grey. She was heading to the kitchen to put the kettle on when the phone rang again. This time it was her publishing agent, Richard Beasley. "Hey, Richard." Julie tried to make her voice sound light and happy. She didn't want Richard to know that the new book wasn't going as well as she would like. She had promised him a draft by the end of the month and it was already the 17th.

"Julie, I'm glad I caught you. I figured you would be hard at it with your phone on silent. I've got some good news. The Board at Tetonkian Romantics have reviewed a couple of your short stories and they are interested in your new book. I told them about your first novel and gave them a copy of that too. They were eager to read it. Sounds promising, huh?" Richard's voice was light and optimistic and made Julie feel better.

"Yes, it does, Richard. Thank you."

"So how's the new book coming? I'm anxious to get it." Richard reminded her.

"Oh, it's coming along. I've had a bit of a delay though. There was an accident with my car." Julie hoped that excuse would suffice.

"Julie, no, are you alright?" Richard's voice changed to concern.

"I wasn't in it. It got sideswiped in the grocery store parking lot. But it's been totaled out by the adjuster and now I have to go car shopping. Can you give me a little extension on that draft?" She didn't want to sound like she was begging but she just didn't seem to be able to get back to writing at the moment. There were too many other things on her mind right now, the car, and of course, Eric Players.

"Oh, I suppose so, but I am anxious to get it and the Board is too. This could be your break to have an established publishing company like ours handle your work. Who knows, you could be the next **Maeve Binchy** if all goes well." Richard hoped he was getting the message to her clearly that she needed to finished her book soon.

"That would be exciting, Richard. I love **Maeve Binchy,** but I could never be as good. I've read all her books. It would be a dream come true to be as successful as she was. As soon as I get another car, I will get back to working on the new book day and night. Promise." She made herself that promise too.

"Well, okay, kiddo, but don't dilly dally too long. We need to see at least a draft. Maybe even a couple of chapters to get them enticed. What do ya say?" Reluctantly, Richard let her go.

"I'll call you soon. Bye." Julie clicked the red button and laid her phone down. She knew she needed to get some pages off to Richard soon since she had received a sizable advance on the new book. But this car problem *and* Eric Players was distracting her. She looked at the phone lying there on the desk and she thought about calling him to ask about his dad. But she remembered the last time she had done that, he had ended the conversation suddenly. She didn't know why or if she had offended or upset him by asking, but she certainly didn't want it to happen again. He seemed to have forgotten about it though when they had *bumped* into each other at the grocery store. And he had been wonderful with taking her to get her groceries at the car repair lot. And their lunch afterwards had been quite enjoyable. They had laughed and talked like old friends. He made her feel so relaxed and at peace. Her usual self-consciousness around people she didn't know well hadn't been noticeable with Eric. So she didn't know why his suggestion of a dinner date with him cooking his Spaghetti Bolognese had scared her.

The car! That was it. He had said he would look online for any possibilities. She should call him and ask him if he would like to go car shopping with her. After all, a man's input and knowledge would be beneficial, she told herself. She knew she could certainly purchase a car without his assistance, but it gave her a good reason to call him. But she hadn't heard from him for three days so maybe he decided against looking because she had turned down his invite to dinner. Her mind was swaying with a whirl of thoughts.

Julie sat with the phone in her hand for almost half an hour as she drank her Earl Grey. 'Should I call? Nope, that wouldn't be proper. But he did say he would help and his input would be helpful. After all, he does drive a BMW. The man certainly knows his vehicles. But can he leave his dad for that long to go gallivanting around the countryside looking for a car for a new neighbor he hardly knows? Nah, it wouldn't be the right thing to do. Yes, but, I like him and I would like to see him.'

Back and forth, back and forth, Julie tormented herself for a few more minutes before she picked up the phone and called. Her heart skipped a little beat when she heard his voice. "Hi Eric, it's Julie, your silly neighbor at the end of the road. How are you?"

"Julie, Hi, I was just thinking about calling you." Eric was truly pleased to hear her voice.

"Really, why?" A warm feeling ran through Julie. He had been thinking about her too.

"Well, I was wondering about how things were coming along with your car repair. I haven't seen you drive by in Red Hot Mama. Were they able to fix her?" Eric was actually hoping the car couldn't be fixed. The idea of car shopping with her was intriguing.

"Nope, she's history. The adjuster totaled her out and the insurance company just called. I'll get a check soon." Julie relayed.

"Oh, that's too bad. I know you really liked that little car. Anyone who names their car Red Hot Mama must really like it." Eric joked.

"You! You're making fun of me again."

"No, I'm not. Remember my car is White Thunder."

"Yes, I remember. And that's why I'm calling you. Umm, this is a bit awkward, you had said you might look online for another car for me. Have you had a chance to look? It's okay if you haven't; I was just wondering if you had found anything. If so, would there be a chance that you would be interested in going car shopping with me and offering some advice on what to get?" Julie let it all spill out quickly hoping she didn't sound too eager.

"Well, yes, I would enjoy that. And yes, I did find a couple of possibilities. You didn't say specifically what you wanted, but I kind of figured since Red Hot Mama was a compact, that you would be open to something similar." Eric had begun the search immediately and was thinking about calling her with his results when she called.

"You certainly have me pegged. Yes, a compact car is just what I want. I would love another Red Hot Mama but I'm sure she will be hard to find. Can you get away for long? How about leaving your dad?" Julie asked concerned, but hoped he would actually consider going with her.

"That's not a problem. There is an on-call home-care nursing group that will come and sit with him while I have to be gone. I've used them once before when I had some business to handle. Let me give them a call and I will get back to you, ok?"

"Sure, that will be great. The insurance check is supposed to come by the end of next week. I'll call you when I get it. Talk to you later, then. Bye."

Julie hung up the phone with a smile on her face. She was going to get to spend time with a very handsome man very soon. Eric Players laid down his phone and a smile came to his face also. He thought about the cute blonde who lived down the lane. He knew he shouldn't be getting involved with a woman at this time, but she was so pretty and he really enjoyed her company. 'What would it hurt?'

Julie headed down the hall back to her office. Suddenly ideas were flowing in her head and her fingers were aching to touch the keys of her laptop. She would have a draft of at least three or four chapters to send off to Richard in no time. The prospect of spending the day with Eric had gotten her romantic ideas bouncing.

Up the street, Eric walked down *his* hall to his dad's bedroom. The machines were humming along quietly and his dad lay peacefully sleeping. Eric wished he could reduce the amount of sedation and have his dad awake for a few hours a day. He really wanted to ask his dad those questions about the accident but he knew it would just end with a heated argument.

CHAPTER 4

    Eric and his dad had worked on many jobs over the years with Eric designing the projects and Ben bringing them to life. Eric had loved being an architect and he missed the feeling of seeing his creations as they started from the ground and rose towards the sky. When he had graduated from college with his degree in Architectural Engineering, his dad had been so proud. He and his dad had loved working together on projects from the time he was a kid. His dad had taught him everything he knew about construction and that had peaked Eric's desire to design buildings. Ben's dream had been to start their own company someday with Eric designing the buildings and Ben handling the construction project.

    That is, before Ben took the job with Streeter Construction. Fred Streeter and Ben Players had been friends for many years, back as far as their college days and Ben had done small projects for Fred when Fred's company was just starting up. They had even talked partnership for a while, but Ben told Fred that he and Eric wanted to start their own company when Eric graduated from college. Fred understood and still asked Ben to head up projects for him whenever he was available. They had had a good working relationship for many years.

When Fred hired Ben to be the construction boss on the Capitol Avenue Apartment project, Eric was a bit concerned. He told his dad that he had heard some *not so flattering* things about Streeter. There were some stories floating around about some of their dealings being a bit shady and Eric didn't want his dad to get caught up in anything like that. Ben had listened but said he didn't believe it. He said he had known Fred Streeter for years, long before Eric went to college. He knew Fred was an honest guy and Ben was certain that the comments about any shady dealings were only made by jealous competitors.

When the Capitol Avenue Apartments project had first been given to Eric to design, he had talked with his dad then because he knew that Streeter Construction probably would be one of the bidders on the job. Eric and his dad had talked about the rumors of inadequate materials and site violations on procedures on recent Streeter projects. Ben said he knew that the Capitol Avenue Apartments was important to his friend. He too had heard that Fred Streeter had dealt with some setbacks lately and that getting the Capitol Avenue Apartments would be a Godsend for his company. There had been talk of some financial troubles, but Ben assured Eric that he was certain his long-time friend would never be involved in anything underhanded just for the money.

So when Eric had completed his design of the building, Ben had reviewed the project with his son and they were both aware of the scope of work that was required to complete it. A thirty-five story high rise building with large luxury apartments, four per floor with underground garage spaces that even had a car wash bay. One hundred and twenty-eight potential tenants with access to full amenities on the first two floors. Game rooms, lounges, a small restaurant/bar, workout rooms, and an Olympic size pool. The penthouse floor would be reserved for corporate guest space for companies to rent. A concierge would be available to all tenants and guests, twenty-four-hour service -- seven days a week. The investor was going all out. The completed building would be magnificent and Eric knew he and his dad would be pleased with his work on it.

It was one of Eric's favorite projects. He was very proud of his design and his boss had been pleased when he saw the semi-final drawings. "Eric, you've outdone yourself here." George Folder, CEO of Folder Architecture and Eric's boss, had said. "This is some of your best work. You just might be seeing a promotion coming out of this when it's done. We are anticipating completion and full occupancy by the end of the year."

Eric had been a little surprised to hear that the investor was expecting full occupancy by the end of the year. It was already late spring by the time bidding started and Eric didn't see how they could possibly complete the project by *next S*pring even. When he had expressed his concern to his dad, it had started the first of their disagreements on the project. Ben was convinced they could get it done in time and Eric was convinced they couldn't. Of course, Streeter did get the bid; his was far below the other bidders who had submitted. Eric was pleased that Streeter had gotten the contract because it meant he would be working with his dad on the biggest project Eric had ever designed, but there was a nagging worry that Streeter might cut corners to get the project done on such a short time frame and within budget. Ben assured Eric that everything would be alright; he would keep a close watch on the project.

Throughout the start of construction, things seemed to be going well, but when the change orders began coming across Eric's desk, he knew that Streeter could be in trouble. He might have bit off more than he could handle. Eric mentioned it to his boss. George hadn't seemed too concerned. He said he had worked with Streeter Construction on smaller projects before and they were a reputable firm. He told Eric not to worry. A few change orders were expected on any project especially one of this size. Eric decided to not say anymore to George, but he intended to keep watching the change orders and visit with his dad about his uneasiness in the building's progress.

A visit to the job site at the end of September made Eric even more concerned about the project being finished by the end of the year. As long as the weather held out, it might be possible, but any inclement days could really put them in a bind. Approaching Fall in Philadelphia, it could go either way.

Ben had made the rounds of the site with Eric and pointed out the progress. Things did seem to be going well. Eric was pleased with almost everything he saw, but he did question the weight of the rebar they were using. Ben assured him that they had used it before in some of his projects and it had done well. The manufacturer stood behind his project, Ben had said. He told Eric not to worry so much, he was on top of it and assured Eric that everything was on schedule. He was certain the building would be ready for occupancy by the end of the year, at least the construction phase. If the interior designers slowed things down, that was not his problem. His duty was to get the structure built and how they decked it out was up to someone else.

Eric had gone back to his office and made notes with regard to his findings that day and the information Ben had supplied. He hoped there wouldn't be any more change orders for a while. There was still an uneasiness in his mind about the concrete support as the building got taller. Thirty-five floors needed strong foundations and each floor needed good rebar for the concrete subflooring. He vowed to visit the job site on a regular basis. He called his dad every few days for updates and it had made Ben mad that his son was checking up on him.

When he had gotten a call that the concrete on the tenth floor had cracked, Eric was concerned that it might not hold. He called his dad immediately to make sure that the construction site was going to be shut down until the inspectors had given approval to proceed. A few days later, Ben had told Eric that everything was alright. He said the inspectors had given their go-head and everyone was busily back at work. The building was now at its twenty-eighth floor and they were moving along quickly. At the rate they were going the topping out ceremony could be mid-November. That left just six weeks for the interior framing and dry wall. It had already been started on the lower floors with the crews working their way up as the structure grew and Ben was pleased that they would be able to keep to the completion time frame. He continued to assure Eric of it, but Eric still had his worries.

When he got the call that there was more trouble at the job site, Eric dropped everything and headed downtown. The sound of the sirens came up behind him and Eric just knew that something bad had happened. He soon found that, his worst fears were realized. With twenty-eight floors of the structure completed, the crack in the concrete on the tenth floor gave way, bringing the entire building crashing down in a cloud of dust and crumpled steel, rebar, concrete and bodies.

Fortunately, it had been an exceptionally windy day and Ben had sent some of the men working on the top floors home early because the progress had been going so well. The workers still on the job site were working on the lower levels installing drywall and they fell with the building as it folded into itself. When Eric arrived, the emergency workers were trying to save some of the men who were dangling from steel beams hanging on for their lives. Others were being taken to nearby hospitals and some were being treated on site. The triage was a nightmare. Workers were scrambling through the debris trying to find anyone who might still be alive. Ambulances were coming and going with the wounded. The entire scene looked like a war zone. Eric frantically asked if anyone had seen Ben Players and he was told there were still several men yet unaccounted for.

Eric grabbed a shovel and fiercely started digging along with the workers nearby. Someone had said they heard shouting from below the rubble so they knew there were some survivors underneath what was left of the luxurious apartment building that had been Eric's dream.

Ben Players was found badly injured along with two of his men who had not survived. The doctors said he probably would recover eventually, but that his injuries might leave him disabled. It would be a long and painful recovery. The broken bones would heal, but the head injury would remain to be seen. Right then and there, Eric promised himself that he would take care of his dad and work to find out the cause of the accident. He prayed that his dad had not been involved in anything that might have caused the collapse.

When the finger had first been pointed to Streeter Construction, Eric knew that his dad would defend Streeter to the bitter end. But with Ben's head injury he was unable to tell anyone exactly what had happened. The lawyers had tried to depose him at the hospital, but Ben's confusion and pain made his speech slurred and his deposition had been contradictory and inadmissible. Eric remembered his concerns about the rebar and the notes he had taken the day of the first walk about with his dad. Of course, when the lawyers began going back and forth as to who was to blame, it had come down to the architectural design being faulty and Eric took the brunt of the consequences for the verdict in spite of the information he shared from his first inspection day earlier on.

Streeter held firmly to their claim that they were using all standard materials and with their chief construction engineer incapacitated, the lawyers agreed to a settlement after long and tiring negotiations. They only way to save both companies were for the architectural design to be determined as faulty. George Folder had apologized to Eric but said it was the only way to save everyone from further liability and lawsuits. Eric knew they were just saving their own butts and didn't care who took the brunt of the blame as long as it didn't affect them.

George Folder told Eric that he would not be able to retain his job nor his license. It was the final settlement made through the lawyers. He would see that Eric had a nice severance package, but that was all he could do. So that was the end of Eric's architectural career and the beginning of his new job as caregiver.

Eric had tried to resume his life in Philadelphia. He didn't plan to look for another job any time soon as the severance package had been substantial. He thought his personal life would be unchanged. But when news of the accident got to his old friends and they found out that Eric had been fired, they looked uncomfortable around him. Eric couldn't give out any details of the settlement and his friends believed that he had been at fault in some way. When Eric refused to explain, they soon refused to return his phone calls to get together and after a few months, Eric reluctantly made the decision to move away from Philadelphia.

CHAPTER 5

Later that week when the insurance check arrived in the mail, Julie called Eric about helping her shop for a new car. "Hi, guess what? My insurance check came today! I guess I'm ready to buy a new car, well not a new one but maybe a little upgrade from Red Hot Mama would be nice. I can't afford a BMW like someone I know," Julie teased.

"No new car? But I thought writers were rich." Eric chided back.

"Yes, if they have a book on the best sellers list, maybe. I haven't been so blessed." Eric had been reviewing available compact cars online and had several good options for Julie to see. "Well, I have some possibilities for us. You didn't say specifically what you wanted, but I had the feeling you were a frugal gal and would be looking for a *gently used*, instead of brand new. I think a one-owner with low mileage, preferably red, of course."

"Ok, that's not fair. We barely know each other and you have me pegged right on." Julie said in amazement.

"Well, at least about cars. There are a couple of decent choices nearby. When shall we go look?" Eric offered.

"We? You're going with me?" Julie was surprised at his suggestion.

"Of course. I thought that was what you wanted. I don't have to physically go but you had asked me to help you *shop*. I just assumed that meant I would make the journey to all the places you wanted to look." Eric made his voice sound like he was a little hurt.

Julie hoped she hadn't upset him. She did want his help or at least to spend some time with him, she admitted to herself. "Oh, yes, I do need you to go with me. You know how they say car dealers are prone to taking advantage of a woman shopping for a used car alone. They all think women know nothing about cars so they can pawn any old thing off on them. They won't try that with a man. It might be different if I was buying new, but a used car salesman does worry me a little." Julie was glad for his help but was mostly thrilled he was going to go with her.

"I'm not sure that old stereotype shyster car salesman still exists. Most of them are pretty reputable, but I am happy to go along and make sure you aren't robbed by a highwayman!" Eric laughed.

"Now you *are* making fun of me. Maybe I will just go buy one alone to show you I can." Julie hoped her pretend disgust wouldn't put him off.

"Alright, alright, enough. Let's set a time and go." Eric wasn't put off in the least. He wanted to spend time with Julie and get to know her better even though the nagging thought in the back of his mind was telling him it wasn't a good idea.

"Tomorrow around 10:00? Is that too soon? You'll need to call the in-home caregiver for your dad, won't you?" Julie asked in anticipation.

Eric's response gave her excited jitters. "I think that should work. Can I call you later to confirm?"

"Sure. Bye." Julie smiled to herself as she laid down her phone. It would be fun car shopping with Eric. 'Oh, who am I kidding? Just spending the day with him would be the fun part'. Getting a new car was the extra icing on the cake. Something about the way they teased each other back and forth, just clicked. She was glad he was a new friend and she would consider possibly something more.

Ten minutes later the phone rang and she reached for it with the anticipation of Eric calling to confirm tomorrow morning, but the contact screen showed *Brandon*. "Hi, Brandon," Julie said into the phone. She was a bit disappointed and her voice must have reflected her feelings.

"What's wrong? Everything okay?" Brandon asked with concern. They had been friends for a long time and he knew her better than she knew herself. He could sense the disappointment in her voice. She just hoped he didn't realize it was because it was him calling instead of Eric.

She and Brandon had been close friends in High School working on the **Screech,** the school paper. Brandon had been the President of the Journalism Club and Julie had joined in the hopes of a career in Journalism. That had changed after she got her first job out of college at the **Journal Gazette** in Fort Wayne and was assigned to writing the obituaries like all new journalists. She soon discovered that Journalism was not going to be her lifelong career. She decided she wanted to write novels.

"Sure, I'm fine. I'm just a bit anxious about shopping for a new car."

"You're tired of Red Hot Mama? I didn't think you would ever get rid of her."

Julie told him all about the accident in the mall parking lot and how Red Hot Mama had been totaled and how she had to find another car.

"Oh, Julie. I'm so sorry. Why didn't you call me? I'll come down and take you." Brandon's tone was his usual voice of concern when anything was wrong with Julie. She did appreciate him and their friendship but she didn't want him to know about Eric Players and their budding relationship. She and Brandon had been friends for so long and Julie sometimes felt that Brandon would have liked it to be more than just friendship. They had dated briefly in High School going to ballgames and the movies and when he asked her to the Senior Prom, she had readily agreed. The evening had been fun dancing under the paper stars in the gym and Brandon had taken her out for breakfast afterwards. It was a magical night. The paper stars had twinkled when the lights were dim and the music was perfect for slow dancing together. The red and blue streamers of their school colors stretched across the room made the ceiling seem like a low and intimate nightclub. They had lingered over breakfast at their favorite diner, DK's in Canterton, and laughed and talked about plans after graduation.

Julie's mom liked Brandon and was agreeable to their relationship and was disappointed when Julie decided not to date Brandon anymore. Julie couldn't quite explain it; it was just something she felt OR didn't want to feel. When Brandon had put his arms around her in the driveway at her house, he leaned in for a kiss and Julie had responded. She had been in anticipation of that kiss for a while. This was the first time Brandon had approached her as more than a friend and she had been hoping he would close their perfect evening with a kiss. She had enjoyed the scent of him as he held her and she snuggled next to him afterwards. He was strong but gentle and he held her with respect even though she could feel his passion. She cared about Brandon and she knew that kiss could be the start of something more than friendship between them and she had felt the warmth go through her body and a gentle tingling all over that frightened her. She had plans that she wasn't sure left room for romance in her life right now. So the next day at school, she broke up with him saying since she was leaving for college and since he was staying in Monique for Junior College, she figured dating long distance would not work.

    Julie knew Brandon had been devastated even though he said he understood and that she probably was right. She promised they would always remain friends and he agreed. So that was what they were. Friends with no benefits other than regular evenings out to dinner and a movie or the theater. Brandon had never married either and she often wondered if he still carried a torch for her but she didn't want to pursue it. No point in bringing up that subject now after so long. Their friendship continued with no talk about that beautiful night at prom, the kiss, and what might have been.

"Thanks, Brandon, but that's not necessary." Julie replied. "I've found a good possibility and will probably buy it today. You don't need to make the trip from Fort Wayne. Thanks, anyway, I can always count on you. I'm sorry I didn't tell you about the accident. It was really nothing and I've had a rental car to get around. I've been busy with the new book, so…." Julie let her hurried explanation trail off.

"Well, ok, then." She could sense he was let down at her not telling him about the car accident and the shopping for a new one.

"The new book is going well." Julie interjected quickly when she heard the disappointment in his voice. "I've had some terrific ideas and I'm about ready to send a draft of the first couple of chapters to Richard. I'm sure he will let you look them over. Oh, look at the time, I've really got to go now. Bye Brandon, love ya."

And with that Julie was gone. Brandon sat with the dead phone in his hand and said to himself, 'I didn't even get a chance to tell her why I was calling. I'll call again tomorrow. She seemed a bit frazzled. Must be the new car purchase.' Brandon had gotten tickets to **Hamilton** and he knew that Julie had been dying to see it. He knew she would be excited when he told her.

Julie had forgotten all about Brandon's call by the time Eric called and confirmed for 10:00 the next morning. She just knew the day would be great. She began to hum softly as she mashed a pot of Earl Grey. It was the perfect time to treat herself to a fresh cup of creamy hot tea and a biscuit as she got back to work on her new book.

The day flew by and Julie did indeed kick out a couple of chapters. She reread through them and decided they were ready for review by Richard. She typed in his email address and attached the pages with a note asking for his response ASAP. She looked at the clock on her desk and realized it was past 6:00 pm. She had worked through the day and hadn't stopped for lunch. A slice of toast when she first got up and the pot of Earl Grey and biscuit was all she had eaten. She pushed herself away from the desk and stretched her arms above her head to get out the kinks in her neck. She was satisfied with what she had accomplished today, but now she needed food! Her stomach growled as she walked down the hallway toward the kitchen. 'What to make quickly,' she wondered. As she peered into the refrigerator, looking at the frozen packages of **Lean Cuisines**, her phone rang.

"Hey, Julie, Eric here. I've made a pot of my special Spaghetti Bolognese and wondered if you would like to join me?"

Julie laughed at the thought of how she was going to make herself a frozen dinner and go to bed. "Eric, you are a lifesaver again. I was just rummaging through my refrigerator trying to decide on something. I've been writing all day. I missed lunch and I'm too tired to make anything. I'm not too tired to eat though and Spaghetti Bolognese sounds wonderful. When do you want me to come?"

"Anytime. The sauce is done and I'm putting the spaghetti in the water to boil. Should only be about 20 minutes. Can you last that long?"

"That would be terrific. I'll try to survive till then. I will freshen up a bit and head your way. Can I bring a bottle of wine?"

"That would be the perfect addition to my homemade spaghetti and special Italian sauce. See you soon." Eric clicked the red button and smiled. A bit of uneasiness churned in his stomach. He knew he shouldn't be getting involved with anyone. If she found out the truth about his dad and the accident, it could bring a lot of trouble his way. But he really liked Julie and decided the risk was worth taking. Maybe the uneasiness in his stomach was hunger. He had been busy cooking all day and hadn't had lunch himself, just a few samples of the sauce as it bubbled on the stove. His grandmother had taught him that recipes were not needed. The finest chefs tasted as they cooked.

Julie hurried to the bathroom to brush her teeth and put on a bit of makeup. She didn't usually bother with makeup on the days she spent writing. Fortunately, she had showered that morning and done her hair. The natural curl in it made it easy to let it dry and pick out for a fluffy **Shirley Temple** look. She checked herself in the full length mirror in the hallway before she grabbed her sweater and the bottle of red wine and headed out the door and up the road.

The sun was beginning to go down and the sky was taking on a beautiful glow behind the trees. The temperature was a balmy 62 degrees; a lovely Spring evening in Indiana. Maybe she would suggest to Eric that they have their supper on the patio and watch the sunset. That certainly would be a romantic setting.

'Whoa, hold it girl! You are sounding like one of your silly romance stories. Getting ahead of yourself there! Knock it off!' Julie chided herself. 'Be just a bit more cautious. You don't know anything about this guy. Yes, but he is so nice and soooo handsome.' Her thoughts fought back and forth all the way up the road. As she rang Eric's doorbell, she shook them away and smiled when he opened the door.

"You are just in time. The pasta is ready and the sauce has been simmering slowly for hours. I hope you are really hungry; I seemed to have made enough for an army. I should call all the neighbors, but I decided I would only call my favorite one. Come, come in. Let me take your sweater."

"I thought maybe supper on your patio might be nice. It looks like we are in for a beautiful sunset. If so, I might need the sweater when the sun goes down completely." Julie offered.

"That's a great idea. I will mix the pasta and sauce and we can take the pan out to the patio if you don't mind that we won't have candlelight and a red and white checkered tablecloth." Eric joked. "I can light the tiki torches though. They are pretty and do help keep the bugs away."

"Let me help. I can take the plates and wine glasses out." Julie had a thought about Eric's father lying in bed down the hall. "Too bad your dad can't join us. It must be so hard having a normal life knowing that his is almost over. What kind of cancer did you say it was?"

Eric felt a moment of panic but answered as calmly as he could. "Some kind of glandular thing; I can't pronounce it. You know doctors and their big words."

"I only ask because I have a good friend, Sarah, from High School who married a doctor, an oncologist actually. He's one of the best cancer doctors in the country. He's at the **Mayo Clinic in Rochester, Minnesota**. I could give Sarah a call and I'm sure she could get you in. He doesn't usually take new patients but for me, I'm sure he would at least listen to your dad's diagnosis and offer his opinion."

"That would have been nice, Julie, but I'm afraid dad doesn't really have much time left and he has a DNR. There'd be no point." He didn't like lying to Julie again, but he just didn't want to talk about the accident.

"I'm sorry, Eric. I shouldn't have brought it up. I just thought…"

"I know you mean well, but I think I have everything under control." Eric changed the topic of conversation as quickly and smoothly as he could. He didn't want to discuss his dad's condition with Julie any further. "Hey, dinner is ready. Let's go eat. I'm starving, how about you?"

"Sounds great." Julie wondered again why Eric always seemed to avoid any discussion about his dad. 'None of my business, I guess. Let it go, Julie,' she told herself.

The evening was delightful. The Spaghetti Bolognese was delicious. Eric said it had been his grandmother's recipe. She was Italian and the list of ingredients had been handed down for generations. He felt very fortunate to know it, but he did pride himself on adding a few extra touches to make it his own secret recipe just like his grandmother had done years ago.

Julie liked the tiki torches. They provided the perfect atmosphere for dinner on the patio and even though there weren't many bugs this early in the season, they lit up the patio with a soft glow. Candlelight and red and white checkered tablecloths were not needed to make it the perfect setting. The evening did turn a bit chilly when the sun finally sank below the trees and disappeared behind the wooded area next to Eric's house. Julie was glad she had brought her sweater and she pulled it tighter around her. "You getting cold?" Eric asked. "We can take our wine and go in. I have a lite dessert. Just a little gelatin with fruit, but the topping is fresh whipped crème I did myself."

Julie laughed. "You are a surprise a minute, Eric Players. That sounds wonderful. Yes, I am a little chilly. Let's go in. I need to use your powder room anyway. Direct me there while you dish up the dessert."

"Second door on the left past my room. Dad is further down the hall. Don't worry about disturbing him, the medication keeps him in a state of sedation, a medical induced coma, I guess you would call it."

Julie headed down the hall as Eric got out dishes for the dessert. She saw the door to Eric's room was open a bit and she looked in. In the corner was a draftsman's table. 'Hmmm, she thought. I wonder why he has that? He's never said what he does for a living. Obviously he works from home. Maybe an architect or engineer of some kind. Must be a good one to afford a BMW and this nice house.'

Eric called from the kitchen. "Dessert is ready; I'll take it to the living room where we can relax with the rest of the wine." Julie finished in the bathroom and hurried back up the hall. She had a couple of questions on her mind. Maybe after the dessert and another glass of wine. She didn't want to pry, but the journalist in her was curious. She would need to ask at some time if they were to continue seeing each other. As she entered the living room, Eric was just lighting the logs in the fireplace. He looked up. "You were chilly so I thought this might help. I'm really glad this house had a gas fireplace; I'm not sure I would be up to cleaning out a real one on a regular basis."

"I think you're right. My auntie in England always told me, 'You wouldn't like fireplaces so much if they were your only heat and you had to clean out the ashes and bring in the wood and start them every day.' She lived in a big old stone farmhouse that had been built in 1833. I loved the fireplaces and always wanted her to build a roaring fire for me even in the summer time. I remember my grandparents toasting hard crusted bread over the fire. Oh, how I loved it with lots of butter when I was a kid." Julie enjoyed sharing her childhood memory with Eric and he smiled as he listened to her.

"Enough talk about me and my childhood. Tell me more about yourself." Julie asked.

"There's not much to tell", Eric answered. "I was an only child. My mom died when I was eight. Dad raised me. It was just him and me so I that's why I'm taking care of him now."

"I noticed when I went to the bathroom that you have a draftsman's table in your room. Are you an architect?"

"What were you doing in my room?" Eric's tone suddenly changed and it startled Julie. "I wasn't *in* your room. The door was slightly ajar when I went down the hall and I just glanced in. I'm sorry." Eric quickly apologized, "No, I'm sorry, I shouldn't have reacted like that. I used to be an architect, but I'm not anymore. It's a long and unpleasant story and one I don't care to remember or go into." His voice sounded tight and curt and Julie realized she had stumbled onto a sore subject. She wanted to know more, but right now was definitely not the time to pursue it. She would wait until they got to know each other better and she would ask again. She changed the topic of conversation. She didn't want to ruin the excellent evening they had been having.

"The Spaghetti Bolognese was fabulous. Your grandmother must have been a delightful cook. Does she still live in Italy?"

Eric was glad she had changed the subject and didn't ask any more questions about his being an architect. "Thank you, no she passed many years ago. I never really knew her well. I was just a kid the couple of times we went. But I loved being in her kitchen. I remember the stone walls and the low wood beams in the ceiling. The smell of sauce on the stove and fresh bread baking in the big stone fireplace. It was wonderful. She would sit me on a tall stool and tell me about whatever it was she was making. I got to sample things as the cooking progressed. It's one of my fondest memories. Later I learned more from the things mom talked about before she died. She had been very close to her mother and I like to think they are cooking together in heaven." Eric had a strange whimsical look on his face and he seemed to have drifted into another place for a moment.

Julie watched him for a moment before she said, "That's a beautiful thought. I'm sure my mom and grandma are making Yorkshire pudding up there too." Eric smiled at her and the tense moment they had earlier was over. The fireplace did indeed present a lot of heat and Julie leaned forward on the sofa to shed her sweater. Eric reached over and helped her with it. For a moment she thought maybe he would take her in his arms and kiss her. Part of her wanted it, but part of her was terrified at the thought. But he just helped her slide her arm out of the sleeve and the moment passed quickly. They continued to talk as they finished the gelatin with the real whipped crème on top. 'Pasta and whipped crème,' Julie thought to herself. 'This guy will make me fat in to time. It's **Lean Cuisine** for the rest of the week.'

"Eric, this has been lovely, but the fire is making me sleepy. My tummy is full and I'm ready for a good night's rest. My brain is wiped from writing all day and now this wine. I should go. Remember we have a full day of car shopping tomorrow." She really didn't want to go and would have liked to see where the evening could have progressed, but she knew that was a territory she didn't need to pursue at the moment. And Eric's mood switches that seemed to come out of nowhere concerned her. He was really a mysterious challenge indeed.

"You are right, my lady. Get some sleep so you will be bright and bushy tailed in the morning. I will pick you up promptly at 10:00 am." Eric walked her to the door and gently placed a kiss on her forehead. "Good night, Julie."

Julie fairly floated down the road to her little cottage. How was she going to sleep now? She could tell that Eric was interested in her. Interested in more than car shopping she was sure, but she was glad he was taking it slow. She wanted to see where this could go but she didn't want to rush into anything. She thought about his sudden moodiness; it was a little off-putting.

She dropped off to sleep instantly in spite of her earlier thought on the way home that she wouldn't be able to sleep thinking about Eric. The full day of writing had certainly worn her out and the mix of pasta and wine had done the rest. She slept soundly all night and when the alarm rang out at eight AM she couldn't believe it! 'Maybe I should forego my evening tea from now on and have wine instead.' The shower felt wonderful. She stood for a while letting the water flow over her body. It was invigorating. Her skin tingled and the excitement of the coming day was on her mind when the phone rang. Her first thoughts were that Eric was cancelling. Maybe something wrong with his dad. She grabbed the phone and saw that it was Brandon. 'Oh, boy, what does he want now?' She didn't want anything to spoil the feelings she was experiencing right now. She hit the green button and said, "Hello?"

"Morning, Julie. I never got to tell you why I called yesterday. You hung up so quickly. Guess what, I have tickets to **Hamilton** for next Saturday night! I know you've been wanting to see it. I spent days trying to get them and then a friend of mine at work. You remember Jayme? He bought the tickets ages ago and now his wife decided she didn't want to go. The baby is due anytime and she didn't think she could sit through the show and is terrified her water will break when she's in public. But that's all the better for us. Aren't you excited?"

Brandon's voice was filled with his own excitement at getting the tickets for the show that Julie had been talking about for months. "That's wonderful, Brandon. Thank you." Julie tried to match the excitement she heard in his voice. Of course, she wanted to see **Hamilton**. But right now, she wished it was with Eric.

"The show starts at 8:00. How about I pick you up at 5:00 and we can go out to eat first? It's only an hour drive back to the city. There's a new restaurant downtown I've been wanting to try. Some of the guys have said it's really good. I know how you like Italian and I hear they have the best Spaghetti Bolognese."

Julie stifled a chuckle. Brandon would be hurt if she said 'No'. She wasn't really that interested in Spaghetti Bolognese after having Eric's awesome homemade pasta and sauce, but Brandon knew it was her favorite Italian dish. He was always so thoughtful. And the tickets to **Hamilton** must have cost a fortune! She hoped Jayme gave him a deal. "That sounds lovely, Brandon, 5:00 it is."

"Bye, Julie, see you next Saturday, love ya." They had often ended their phone conversations with 'love ya'. And she did love Brandon. He was the best friend she had ever had. And she did love spending time with him. Over the years they had shared many evenings over delicious meals and good conversations. They had watched dozens of Broadway plays together and all the Oscar nominated movies. Wandering through museums was a passion they shared often. She couldn't imagine a better time than what they had throughout the past sixteen years.

He had sat with her and held her while she cried when her mom died and then again over her first rejection letter. And the second and the third and several more after that. He encouraged her not to give up on her writing. He said she would be a success someday. He believed that with all his heart. Then he had celebrated and held her again as she cried tears of joy over her first check for a short story she had sold! He then gave the story to his boss to read and helped her get her first full romance novel published by a small local publisher.

Brandon's boss, Richard Beasley, had been impressed with that book and gave Julie a substantial advance on her new book, confident that she would have a best seller because Brandon had said so. Yes, she owed a lot to Brandon. He was truly a wonderful friend and she would never want to hurt him. But if things worked out with Eric, she was going to have to tell Brandon that they wouldn't be going out on these regular *dates* anymore. She wasn't sure how she would tell him. She was grateful to him for all the years of friendship and truly looked forward to next Saturday for dinner and the play. They had grown close over the years; she truly loved him. But Brandon had never indicated he wanted anything more since the one kiss after Prom, and their leaving for College, so they remained just friends. It was an unusual relationship, but it seemed to work well for them. Neither one had made any advances in changing it. She often wondered why.

Julie shook those thoughts of Brandon out of her head. Today was car shopping with Eric. She could mask her feelings with Brandon when they went to see **Hamilton**. But now, she was getting ready for a delightful day with Eric.

CHAPTER 6

"Hi Sunshine," Eric said as she got into his BMW the next morning. "Are you ready to shop 'til you drop?"

"Oh, my gosh, I hope it doesn't take that long." Julie couldn't imagine it. She didn't like shopping of any kind. She did hope to spend most of the day with Eric, but car lot after car lot didn't appeal to her much. Her plan was to find a suitable vehicle at a reasonable price, buy the thing and then spend the rest of the day and evening with a meal and perhaps a walk in the park. Or maybe a visit to the new museum that had opened in Canterton. It was only a half hour drive from Monique and they could stop there before they went home. She had heard reports that it was quite the place for history and antique buffs. She didn't know if Eric was into that sort of thing, but she always enjoyed those places because they gave her inspiration for her writing. Brandon had promised to take her sometime soon but they just hadn't scheduled the date.

Museums required at least a half day if not all day, to see everything. She loved reading the little signs at each exhibit if there was no docent to take them through. She and Brandon had talked about going weeks ago, but her writing and his work had kept them from scheduling a full day to really enjoy it. She thought, 'We can always go another time even if I do stop there with Eric today'. She never tired of visiting museums over and over again. There were always new displays and even the old ones can sometimes have something that catches your eye you didn't see before and a different docent might have a tidbit to share that another did not. She hoped Brandon wouldn't be mad that she had seen it without him. 'Maybe best not to mention it,' she decided.

"It's a beautiful day and I'm ready to look at cars, how about you?" Eric's smile would have made any day beautiful and Julie was definitely ready.

"So did you find some good bargains for me?" She asked as she fastened her seatbelt. Eric's car was magnificent and she could never dream of having one like it, but at least she hoped she would find one she just *had* to have! And if it happened to be the first one she looked at, all the better. Shopping done; on to the fun part of the day!

"As a matter of fact, I did. There is a Nissan I thought you might like and an older Chevy Sonic just like Red Hot Mama, but it might have a few too many miles and it was a four-owner." Julie didn't like the sound of that. She had bought Red Hot Mama brand new and the idea of four other people's butts sitting in it didn't appeal to her. "I think I will pass on even looking at that one. You just never know what it's been through with that many owners. If I have to chip in a bit more money, I'd rather have a newer model that's just had one owner."

"What about this Nissan; looks good, here." Julie took his phone and looked at the picture and the info that Eric had found online. "Well, it looks okay, but I don't know much about Nissans and I really liked my little Chevy Sonic."

"I kind of thought so too. I was looking online this morning and I saw a 2018 Chevy Sonic, four door hatchback, grey interior. One owner, low mileage. They are asking $12,500 for it. It's in Newhall and that's about a two-hour drive, but it does sound like a good option. Unfortunately, it's not red. It's white."

"That does sound reasonable. I wasn't planning to spend much more than the $9,700 insurance money, but I probably can't find anything for that price that's worth anything. Besides that, the car rental place is costing a fortune, it probably will make my insurance go up. I think I can manage the difference for the Sonic. I transferred some money from savings yesterday, so I should have enough in my checkbook. If you're sure you don't mind that long of a drive, I'm game."

"Let's do it. Sounds like fun." Eric smiled at Julie and he realized this was the first time in a long time that he had felt like smiling and this beautiful lady in his car was the reason. He knew it was going to be a good day.

The conversation flowed easily on the two-hour drive to Newhall. The farmers were in their fields plowing and planting and they enjoyed the scenery along the way. Julie commented on the lovely farmhouses and said she had always wanted to live in the country.

"Not me. I'm a city boy. Moving here from Philadelphia was quite an adjustment. I lived in a condo in a high rise downtown. Monique is certainly different. Sometimes our cul-de-sac is way too quiet. I loved the nightlife in the city and there doesn't seem to be that much to do here."

"What do you mean? Of course there is, if you look for it. There's the park and the walking trail that runs close to our houses. The community pool is only about 4 blocks away. Southern Hills Junior College offers wonderful adult classes. Oh, but you probably couldn't get away that easy with taking care of your dad, huh?"

"Oh, that's not a problem. I can hire the caregiver like I did today, but I never know where to look for activities. I guess I'm kind of a loner."

"We have an excellent library and a community theatre group that puts on at least three productions a year and they are terrific, as good as anything you would see in Fort Wayne. And of course, Fort Wayne is only an hour drive and there are lots of things to do there. Delicious restaurants and theatres. Museums and concerts. I never tire of going."

"You sound like an ambassador for the Chamber of Commerce." Eric chuckled.

"Sorry, I guess I just love my hometown."

"Hmmm, well, you might convince me. Like to show me around sometime?"

"Of course, I'd love to. We may be small, but mighty." Julie joked. "Tell me more about Philadelphia. What do you do as an architect?" Julie felt like this was the perfect opportunity to ask about Eric's occupation again.

Eric hesitated and there was a long moment of silence before he answered. "I don't really talk about it much. I *was* an architect there, but I'm not anymore."

"Why not? You must have been good at it to afford this nice car and your lovely house." Julie thought that he was about to open up, but he changed the subject again and very firmly said, "I don't want to talk about me and my failed career. Why don't you tell me more about you and yours? When did you know you wanted to be a writer and how did you get started?"

She was pleased that he wanted to know more about her and her budding career since it was obvious he didn't want to talk about his. The tone of his voice had said more than his actual words. So Julie decided not to ask anything further. If he wanted to share, it would be fine. She didn't want a repeat of last night's awkwardness even though it had only been brief. But that didn't stop her from being curious. 'Maybe it had something to do with his dad. I suppose he had to give up his job to take care of his dad. That must be it, and he was uncomfortable talking about it. People probably made too much of his sacrifice.' She didn't want to do that either, so she kept the topics light and fun. They talked about their favorite movies and music. Their cooking abilities or lack thereof! Eric promised to make his famous or was it infamous chili? That and the spaghetti were his only triumphs in the kitchen. Julie reminded him that soup and sandwich were her go-to meals.

"But what about the roast and Yorkshire pudding you mentioned? That sounds a bit more industrious than soup and sandwich."

"Oh, I forgot I told you about that. Yes, well, having my British ancestry, I had to learn how to make it or I would be drummed out of the family. It's really not that difficult."

"I like pudding, what flavor do you make? Eric asked innocently.

Julie let out a big guffaw. "It's not a dessert pudding!"

"It's not, well what is it? Pudding is pudding, just different flavors, right?"

"Not in England, I guess. Yorkshire pudding is more of a pastry that you eat with your meat and potatoes and gravy."

"What? That sounds weird."

"No, it's not, silly. It's just an egg, milk and flour batter that you pour into the meat drippings from the roast and bake it. It rises up and becomes crispy around the edges. It's then cut into pieces and you pour gravy over it. It's quite lovely."

"It sounds a bit different, but good?" Eric wasn't sure he wanted gravy on his pudding, crispy or not.

"Delicious. It's a must with a roast on Sunday. I will make it for you sometime. You'll love it." The easy chatter had continued and they were in Newhall in no time. The two hours had passed incredibly quickly. The car dealership was a large one. There were lots of people wandering around looking at the cars. Julie hoped the Sonic was still there. "Do you see it? I hope no one has taken it."

"Don't worry, I called them before we left and asked them to hold it for us. I had a feeling that this is the one for you."

"But if it isn't, won't they be mad? What if they missed out on another chance to sell it? You shouldn't have done that. I'm surprised they would even consider doing it."

"I promised the salesman his commission regardless of your decision."

"You didn't do that! No!" Julie exclaimed.

"I'm not worried. I think this will be it." Laughed Eric.

Eric was right. When Julie saw the car, she loved it instantly. The test drive was hardly necessary, but they did take it for a short spin down the highway. The mileage was only 22,200 and it had the backup camera and remote start just like Red Hot Mama. Julie managed to talk the salesman down a couple of hundred dollars and the deal was made. She wrote a check and he asked them to wait while he went to get the paperwork completed. He said their sales manager would be with them shortly. So they waited. And they waited. People came and went. More people walked in and visited with salesmen. They even saw *their* salesmen dealing with someone else.

Another couple who had come into the showroom *after* Julie and Eric was already in the office and were happily signing their paperwork and laughing with the manager. Julie was not happy with the lack of prompt service.

It was past 1:30 by then and both of them were getting hungry for some lunch. Julie was losing patience and just when she was ready to go to the counter and say, 'forget it, just give me back my check and I'll go somewhere else and buy a different car', the salesman came over with a box of pizza in his hand and offered them a slice while they waited. He was sorry it was taking so long but it shouldn't be much longer; they were a bit short handed in the office today. The pizza was hot from the store and the slices were large and very cheesy. It filled the void in their hungry stomachs and calmed Julie's disdain for how long they had been waiting. When they had finished eating, the office manager gave them a wave to join him in his office. He said the paperwork was ready and ushered them to the two chairs in front of his desk where the other young couple had been moments before. He apologized again for the wait and Julie suggested to him that they needed to have another manager on staff to handle more than one customer at a time. The office manager smiled and apologized; saying they had been pretty busy that morning and there had been a delay in the wash bay getting her car ready. A half hour later they were ready to hit the road for home with Julie's new car and she felt the tension and anger starting to leave her body.

It had been cleaned up nicely and her salesman gave Julie basic instructions on the accessories. She thanked him, but didn't really feel it; she just wanted the keys and to be on the road. Time with Eric was already being wasted and they had the long drive home in separate vehicles. "I didn't think we would ever get out of there! I'm so sorry you had to sit and wait. I seriously was ready to cancel the deal."

"I could tell. Patience is not one of your virtues?" Eric teased.

"I told you I didn't like shopping, now you know why. They are always right there to convince you to buy, but fall short when it comes to finishing the task. It's the same way in department stores, the floor sales girl follows you around trying to help, but when you get to the counter with your purchases, it's the waiting game again. I hate it." The anger was rising again as she talked about it.

"Calm down; it's done and we are ready to go. So, do you want to take the lead or shall I?" Eric asked.

"You go ahead, I'll follow. Hey, do you want to stop at that museum I mentioned in Canterton? We'll be almost home by the time we get there and I know of a great little diner in town where we can get supper afterwards. Dear friends run it, Dave & Karen Wilson. It's called DK's Diner. I've been going there since High School." She didn't mention that it had always been with Brandon. "The salesman's pizza was good, but not enough to last me all evening. What do ya think?"

"Ummm, sounds okay, but let me warn you, I am not much of a history or antique buff. I can manage maybe an hour walking around looking at the displays then I'm outta there. Kind of like you with shopping." Eric was not fond of museums but knew he could tolerate if it would help get Julie in a better mood.

"Deal. I'm sorry I was such a grouch. We can catch an early supper after the museum. I'll be following you 'til we get to Canterton, then I'll pass you at the edge of town and lead the way to the museum. I put the address in my phone GPS."

"Sounds good. See you in an hour and a half. I'll call the house and let the caregiver know I will be a little longer."

Eric thought about Julie as she drove off. She was quite a woman. One that he could really be interested in pursuing a longer relationship with, but he also knew that now was really not the right time. Taking care of his dad and finding out more details on the building collapse were the most important things in his life right now and he didn't want to involve anyone else in that, especially someone as sweet as Julie. They waved to each other as they pulled out of the dealership lot.

Julie was pleased with the way her new car handled. Well, she knew it wasn't brand new, but it felt like it and the salesman had sprayed that new car smell stuff in it. She decided she wouldn't miss Red Hot Mama, but she did miss the extra $2,600 she had to pay for this one. 'Oh, well, it's only money and you can't take it with you.'

The drive seemed to fly by. Julie sang along with some of her favorite songs on the radio. She had asked the salesman to tune it in for her and set her favorite station. Eric had been watching in his rearview mirror checking to see that she was still behind him and he could see her singing. It brought a smile to his face. The shopping face was gone and he felt the rest of the day would be good as long as they didn't spend too much time at the museum. At the edge of Canterton, Julie pulled around Eric and honked. He waved back and followed her to the museum parking lot. As they got out of their cars, he asked, "So how does she handle?"

"Great! I love it. Thank you so much for finding it for me."

"I saw that the radio was working well."

"Oh, no you saw me singing? Well, thank goodness you couldn't hear me!"

"What? Singing not one of your many talents?" Eric enjoyed their friendly teasing. It had been a long time since he had felt so comfortable with a woman. "So what's her name?"

"Who? Oh, you mean my car!" Julie blushed; a little embarrassed. She hadn't really given it much thought on the drive home. Her thoughts were more about the man in the car in front of her. "Well, you already have taken White Thunder, hmmm, how about Stormy? It's appropriate since she's white, you found her for me, and I found *you* wandering around my house on a stormy night. I think it's the perfect name for my new little lady."

Eric laughed. "You are a writer for sure!" He reached for Julie's hand and said, "Ok, let's go look at some antiques!" Julie liked the feel of her hand in his even though she had been surprised when he took it. Maybe he was just being a gentleman as they crossed the street, because he let it go as they climbed the stairs of the stately old building.

The museum was nice and Eric seemed to enjoy the exhibits. It was all about the history of coal mining in Indiana. There was a replica of a mine that you could ride an old coal cart down the rails into what looked like the depths of the mine from the early 1830s. The sign explained that surface mining didn't become common until after the 1920s up until the 1970s, when they again began using underground mines. The cart was automated, not pulled by a mule as they did in the 1800s. It was more like an amusement park ride, but Julie thought it was fun to sit in the dark with Eric next to her. After the ride through the mine, the docent was knowledgeable about the other displays as she talked about how 97% of Indiana coal was used to generate electricity today rather than for fuel for steamboats and railroad engines like the 1800s. It was interesting and Julie managed to stretch the hour she had promised Eric into an hour forty-five. There didn't seem to be any complaints from him and when they were wandering through the Gift Shop on the way out, they realized they were both hungry for some food.

"How about that diner you mentioned? That slice of pizza is long gone." Eric whispered to her. "I am beginning to feel faint from lack of nourishment and all this walking back into history."

Julie gave his arm a little push and said, "You'll survive. Come on then; get ready to eat the best cheeseburger you've ever had. That is if you can walk 3 blocks down the street to DK's."

"I don't know. If I pass out, will you do CPR?" Eric teased.

The burgers were consumed over a piping hot pile of onion rings they shared. Julie had ordered a double platter and they both dived into the thin crispy pieces of coated onion while they waited for their burgers. A half bottle of ketchup later, they were wiping their fingers and their mouths. "That was the best supper ever!" Eric said as he wadded the napkin into ball and put it on the red and white checkered tablecloth. I did *not* know about this place, but I'll definitely come here again!"

"Did you save room for dessert? They have the best ice cream too."

"Oh, no. No can do. I will burst if I eat another bite. Can we do this again sometime though? I will order the Junior burger next time so I can leave room for the ice cream. And you, my lady, why did you order the double platter of onion rings?" Eric chastised.

"They were good, huh?" I've been coming here for years and I never get tired of their food. You said you were starving and I wanted my fair share of onion rings, so I figured I'd better order a double."

"How did you find this place? I don't think they do much advertising. I've never seen anything about it in the local shopper. It looks like it's just a hangout for the locals."

"I know; they've been here for a long time. People know about it so they really don't need to advertise." Julie was hesitant to mention Brandon. But, after all, Brandon was her best friend and Eric should understand that. "My high school buddy, Brandon Jenkins, brought me here when we were in school. We didn't have much money back then and this place has always been very reasonable. Their prices haven't changed much in the past twelve years." She was glad she had mentioned Brandon because when Karen, their waitress, brought the ticket, she said, "Hey, Julie, good to see you; where's Brandon? And who's your new friend?"

"Karen, this is Eric Players, my new neighbor. He lives down the road from me and he helped me find a new car today. Red Hot Mama, poor thing, was in an accident."

"Oh, dear, you ok? I hope you weren't hurt."

"No, I'm fine, but Red Hot Mama not so much. It was a hit and run in the mall parking lot."

"Geez, some people." Karen handed the ticket to Eric and walked away shaking her head. "Say hi to Brandon for me." Eric quickly took the ticket to the counter and headed to the counter to pay. "You were right, their prices are as amazing as the food," he said to Julie as they walked back to their cars.

"I told you. Thanks for supper and thanks for the great day and thanks for helping me find Stormy. And you should have let me buy supper."

"Nope." Eric shook his head defiantly.

"Well, you definitely will have a roast and Yorkshire pudding in your future then."

"I was hoping so," he laughed.

"Ok, then. I'm going to head for home. I've got to do some laundry before bedtime. See ya later." Julie got into her new car and pulled onto the highway. She glanced in the rear view mirror and saw Eric waving as he climbed into his BMW. She really liked Stormy even though it wasn't as luxurious as Eric's car. It was the perfect fit and she was glad Eric had found it for her. She smiled to herself and hummed along with the music all the way home.

Spot was waiting for her at the garage door as she came into the kitchen. He was meowing and she picked him up for a snuggle. "Hey big boy, did you miss me? You don't like it when

I'm gone all day, huh? Well, guess what; we have a new car to ride in. Hope you like it as much as I do. Come on, let's go get some kibble snacks for you." Spot meowed happily now that Julie was home and cuddling with him. He followed Julie around as she gathered up the laundry and started the washer. There were a few dishes in the sink from breakfast and her snack the night before so she washed them up. No need to start the dishwasher for just a few things. Might as well do them while the laundry is going. There was only one big load and the laundry was done by 10:30 and she was just folding the last of the towels when the phone rang. 'Who is that at this hour?' When she looked at the phone, Richard Beasley's name was on the screen. "Richard, what are you doing calling this late?" Julie answered in surprise.

"Sorry, I wasn't thinking about the time. Hope I didn't wake you. I just finished reading and Julie, I just had to tell you that I love the chapters you sent. They are terrific. I can hardly wait 'til you finish it. It feels like your best work and I know the Board will want to publish it. This could be the one that brings you stardom!"

"Really? Richard, that's awesome. I've been working on it every day as I promised. I do appreciate that extension you gave me. I was having a hard time getting started, but once I did, the ideas just came flowing. I even had a couple of brilliant ones hit me while I was in the shower. I could hardly wait to dry off and get to my office."

Richard laughed. "I would have loved to see that. No, wait, I didn't mean that. Damn, that sounded inappropriate. Forgive me, Julie. I just got caught up in your excitement. Send me the next few chapters when they are ready. When I get about half of it, I will start editing. I'm thrilled it's going so well for you. Again, sorry for my stupid remark. Talk to you again soon. Bye."

He had hung up so quickly, Julie didn't have time to tell him not to worry about the silly comment. She knew what he meant. Richard Beasley was in his 60's, bald and a bit overweight, but an all-round nice guy. Julie knew he hadn't meant anything by what he said. She had met him last year after Brandon had given him her first batch of short stories to critique.

Tetonkian Romantics was hosting a party for one of their authors who had just made the best sellers list and Brandon had introduced her to Richard and his lovely wife, Natasha. They had spent the evening chatting at their table. It was so nice of Richard to invite her and Brandon to join their party. He had introduced her as the newest *up and coming* author to join the ranks at Tetonkian. She was very pleased with that introduction especially since they had been relying on Brandon's recommendations after reading her short stories. She felt the glow of the compliment all evening. She was optimistic about the association with Tetonkian Romantics; it was going to be a good one. Having Brandon faithfully promoting her was going to make it really special and she was glad that she and Richard had developed a good working relationship immediately.

CHAPTER 7

Saturday morning, Julie woke up to rain and a miserable looking overcast day. Spring in Indiana. 'April showers bring May flowers, they always say.' Julie looked out her office window as she sipped her first cup of tea of the day. The daffodils were beginning to bloom and it looked like a couple of voluntary tulips from the previous owner were coming through the ground. And there was just a hint of the peony stems popping up that she had planted last year. A friend had given her some shoots and although she wasn't a gardener, she had managed to dig a few holes along the edge of the yard right at the tree line of the wooded area.

If they survived, she hoped to have a few lovely blooms by Memorial Day. She remembered her American grandma cutting peonies and irises to take to the cemetery every year. It was a family tradition, one that Julie didn't necessarily share the joy or commitment. She had told her mom that she wouldn't do it. She would send her flowers while she was alive, but there was no point in putting flowers on a grave where sightless eyes lay. It was a waste of time and money.

They had argued about it many times and Julie had held firm to her beliefs even though it had hurt her mother's feelings. Now that her mom was gone, Julie did feel compelled to visit the cemetery with a bunch of artificial flowers purchased from the store every once in a while. She was sure her mother would be happy to see them even if they were plastic. It wasn't an annual event for her, but occasionally the desire to walk to the cemetery came over her. Maybe she would take some peonies this year if they bloomed. She would have preferred to plant a peony bush on site, but the cemetery no longer allowed plantings at the grave sites as they had years ago. Too bad really, there were some beautiful peonies at some of the older graves. Julie understood why the groundskeepers didn't enjoy having to mow around bushes and trees since the gravestones were hazardous enough. But she knew her mom would have loved a peony bush blooming every year. Julie would have planted it right there between her mom and dad.

The rain continued throughout the morning but began to let up by noon. Julie was relieved. She didn't relish going to the theatre in Fort Wayne in pouring rain. When Brandon called to confirm the time to pick her up, she had said, "Let me meet you at the restaurant. With this rain, there's no reason for you to drive an hour here to get me and an hour back. And another 2 hours to bring me home later. Who knows, the storm might get worse."

"But I always come to get you, Julie. It's no bother. A gentleman should always call for his date. That's what my grandmother taught me. And the rain is supposed to be done by noon. And if it does get worse later in the evening, I don't want you driving home in it alone."

"Really, Brandon, you worry about me too much. I prefer to meet you there. I haven't had Stormy out of town since I got her and I would enjoy the drive." Actually, Julie was thinking she didn't want Eric to see Brandon picking her up. And besides she thought, 'maybe I should begin stretching the ties between me and Brandon a little to let him down easier if Eric should actually develop into something. I don't want to abruptly break off seeing Brandon; his friendship means too much to me, but he will have to understand if I have someone else in my life.'

"It's only been a week since you got your new car." Brandon protested.

"Yes, and I want to drive her." Julie was adamant.

"Well, if you insist. I don't get you sometimes, Julie, you can be as stubborn as an old mule. If you want to make the drive yourself, fine, meet at the restaurant; it's on Riverview Avenue next to the old amusement park grounds. You know where I mean? It's called Chamberlain's."

"Who you calling an old mule? You, grumpy goose!" Julie tried to make light of her insistence on his staying in Fort Wayne. "Chamberlain's? I thought you said it was an Italian cuisine restaurant? Chamberlains isn't exactly Italian that I know of."

"It is an Italian restaurant; Maria Stefanio is the co-owner and chef. She married Marshall Chamberlain and his folks gave them the money to start the place so they thought they should name it for them. I know, weird, but that's it. The food is to die for though. I had lunch there with Richard a couple of weeks ago. We really enjoyed it and I think you will too."

"Maria Stefanio, isn't she Benjie and Jonita's daughter who used to run **BJ's Restaurant & Brewhouse** downtown Fort Wayne?"

"Yep, after her folks died, she sold **BJ's** and bought this place with her husband. They used her money from that sale to completely remodel the inside after Chamberlain bought it. And you should know, the cheese curds are just as good as they were at **BJ's**. I asked Maria about the recipe and she said, "I cannot tell you. It was Mama and Papa's recipe and it must stay with me as Mama and Papa wanted." Brandon attempted to relate Maria's words with an Italian accent without much success. Julie laughed.

"Oh, gosh, I remember them from college. They were crispy on the outside and when you bit into one, it filled your mouth with the soft gooey melted cheese. Yummy. It's making my mouth water just talking about them. Alright, then. I will meet you at Chamberlain's at 6:00. I'll be working on the new book the rest of the morning till early afternoon, so you'd better have your checkbook with you or your credit card, because I will be hungry by then, if I don't stop for lunch!"

"No problem; I guess I'll have to wash dishes if you overeat my credit limit; I'll see you there. Set an alarm so you don't get wrapped up in your new book and lose track of time. Bye, love ya."

Julie smiled. Brandon was such a great guy. She wondered why he had never found anyone. After they had decided to just be friends, she had hoped he would find someone. She knew he had been focused on his career in publishing, but Tetonkian Romantics didn't seem like a high pressure employer. Richard was easy to get along with; Brandon had often talked about Richard

Beasley's relaxed personality and the casual work environment. Surely there had been some single gals who worked there to take an interest in him. A little flirting might do him some good. She might suggest it to Richard and see what he has to say.

Brandon wasn't movie star handsome, but he kept his sandy brown hair in a pleasing style and she knew he worked out regularly to maintain his slim, yet muscular physique. In addition, he rode his bike to work every day. He said it was to help save the environment, but she knew he enjoyed getting a tan during the summer months. The sun would bleach out his hair and turn his skin a delicious light tan and she had to admit he looked quite fetching in a pair of shorts and a T-shirt or swim trunks. Surely there was someone at Tetonkian who had noticed.

Julie thought about how they had spent many summer weekends at Brandon's beach cabin on Lake Ferrell. Next to her own cottage, it was one of her favorite places because Brandon made it that way. She thought how they would make plans during the middle of the week and Brandon would pick her up early on Saturday and they would not return 'til late Sunday night. The lake was only a half hour drive south of Monique. Brandon had purchased the cabin when he got his first promotion at Tetonkian. The bonus check covered the down payment and the first year of the mortgage. Brandon had made extra payments and had it paid off free and clear in a few years. She remembered how excited he had been when he told her he wanted to purchase it. He had taken her to look at it with him. It was a lovely little log cabin. Well, actually, it was one of those pre-fab log homes, but it looked like a traditional log cabin on the outside. The people who had built it had done an excellent job of finishing it and unless you looked really hard, you would never know it was pre-fab.

It had two small bedrooms, with a full bath between, a little efficiency kitchenette, and an amazingly ample living room. The living room had a huge stone fireplace, with a wide wooden mantle perfect for hanging Christmas stockings. Julie had always said that's what she would do, if she lived there year round. The cabin didn't look very large from the outside. It was dwarfed by the surrounding trees, so Julie had been surprised when Brandon took her to see it. She hadn't known what to expect but when she went inside, she fell in love with it instantly.

Julie especially loved the huge stone fireplace and told Brandon he would have to build her a fire whenever they were there. She had insisted on a fire every Saturday evening, no matter how warm the day had been. And it did seem like the breeze from the lake cooled the cabin after the sun went down. Brandon never objected; he knew how Julie loved a fire in the fireplace. He made sure there were plenty of logs on hand. A neighbor's boy had been chopping them for him for several years and Brandon enjoyed not having to do the work himself. He was capable of it, of course, but he preferred to spend his time with Julie rather than chopping firewood all Saturday afternoon.

Afternoons were spent hiking down the steep hill to the lake's edge and the *beach*, a luxury that no one else at Lake Ferrell had. Brandon had paid a guy to clear the ground and bring in a couple of truckloads of sand to make a beach. He and Julie loved to swim and sunbathe. She had been a lifeguard at the city pool in high school and she insisted that summers were meant for swimming. Brandon made sure there was enough sand to make the beach and then extended it on into the water's edge so that you didn't have to walk into the soft gooey mud as you entered for a swim. So Julie had dubbed it the *beach cabin* even though it was just a log cabin, near a lake in a wooded area in southern Indiana, with no ocean in site.

The tree line ended at the sandy area and gave just enough shade for picnics after swimming and sunbathing. It was the perfect place to spend a summer day. Later they had to make the strenuous climb back up the hill to the cabin, but it was worth it. They kept marshmallows, graham crackers and Hersey bars in the cupboard to make s'mores at least once or twice each summer and after the post beach climb, a little sugar energy was needed.

In the evenings they would sit in the big antique wooden rocking chairs in front of the fire with a glass of wine and listen to music on the old time gramophone that Brandon had found in an antique shop. The records that came with it were scratched a bit, but it made this delightful swishing sound as it played the old tunes from the early 1900s. The creak of the old rocking chairs on the wood floor added to the peaceful ambience. Julie had found them the first summer after Brandon had purchased the cabin. She had just been browsing with no intention of making a purchase when she saw them at the back of the store. They were high backed with wide seats and Julie knew they would be the perfect addition to the living room in front of a roaring fire where they would make s'mores to eat with their after-dinner wine. After a day of swimming or boating or just lying in the sun before a picnic and evenings in those old chairs had become the most restful end to a day anyone could imagine. Lovely memories that Julie felt a little sad about and knew she would miss if she and Brandon didn't continue their friendship after she developed a relationship with Eric. It might prove to be an awkward situation.

Julie put aside the reminiscing and got back to work. The afternoon went by quickly and she managed to kick out several more pages of her new book. It was coming along really well. She wanted to keep working, but she decided she better quit by 4:00 to get ready for her evening out with Brandon. By 5:00 PM, Julie had showered and washed her hair. She fixed her makeup and put on the blue velveteen suit she had purchased recently at the thrift store at the mall. It had been another impulse purchase, not one she would usually look at but the price was incredible. She didn't know how they could do business there with the low prices. The suit looked like it had never been worn and the price tag was marked down to $4.50! It would have been ten times that new in a retail store! The blue color matched her eyes and brought out their sparkle. She had been thinking she would wear it when she saw Eric the next time, but he hadn't asked her on a real date as of yet. And the suit was the perfect thing to wear to the theatre. A silk scarf with tiny yellow flowers on it was the perfect complement to the blue velveteen and she was pleased with her reflection in the hall mirror.

She reached for her clutch, her phone, and grabbed her car keys from the hook on the wall near the door. As an afterthought, she headed to the front hall way and pulled out the umbrella with the spikey end, just in case the weather changed. Her thoughts drifted back to the rainy night she had met Eric and had wielded the umbrella as protection against the possible intruder. She laughed to herself as she opened the garage door and backed Stormy out to meet Brandon at Chamberlain's in Fort Wayne.

Brandon was waiting for her at a lovely table with a white tablecloth and candles and a live pink carnation in a tall skinny vase. It was a beautiful restaurant and she hoped the food was as good as the décor. Brandon had ordered a bottle of her favorite Cabernet. She knew that it was expensive and said, "How lovely, Brandon, but the wine wasn't necessary. We don't want to be too inebriated to enjoy the show." She joked.

"I know, but this is a special night. You are finally getting to see **Hamilton**. You look beautiful. Is that a new suit? I like it. It matches your eyes."

"Thank you, yes. And the scarf you gave me for my birthday last year goes wonderfully, don't you think?"

"Absolutely; it's perfect. Are you hungry? I know I am. I've been here about a half hour and the aromas from the kitchen have been driving me crazy."

Julie looked at her watch. "Am I late?" Julie knew she wasn't always on time and that it irritated Brandon.

"No, no, I just wanted to be here to get a good table. I thought it would be busier. They don't take reservations. But, I would imagine once people learn about this place, they will have to start." Brandon had risen to pull out Julie's chair and he gave her shoulders a little hug as she sat down. Julie was a bit surprised. It wasn't like Brandon to be touchy feely. He must be as excited about the play as she was.

The meal was as good as anticipated; although Julie had decided against the Spaghetti Bolognese. "But that's your favorite." Brandon had protested when she said she wanted to look over the menu for something else.

"I know, but I'm thinking I will try something different. We can have Spaghetti Bolognese anytime. I wonder what they consider their house special?" She didn't want to tell Brandon about the delicious Spaghetti Bolognese she had just experienced at Eric's. After perusing the extensive menu, she decided on the steak Florentine with the marinated mushroom sauce and polenta. "And a side salad with your house dressing," she told the waiter.

"Well, you must be hungry! Save room for the dessert though I hear it's heavenly. I don't care what you say, I'm having the Spaghetti Bolognese." Brandon said. "I've been thinking about it all week. Richard came here with Natasha last week and they loved it."

They talked comfortably over dinner and Brandon poured another glass of wine finishing off the last of the Cabernet when their Tiramisu was brought to the table. "Oh, my!" Julie exclaimed after the first bite. "This *is* to die for!"

"I know. I've been told that. I'm glad you are enjoying it."

"Yes, but I won't be getting into my bathing suit any time soon. I need to get my bike out and do a few miles to take off these calories. Summer is just around the corner and I need to get ready. I've been spending too much time at the computer on the new book. Writing doesn't give you much exercise, except for the fingers. I probably have the skinniest fingers in town!"

Brandon laughed. "That reminds me, I'm going to open the beach cabin for the season. I need to get it ready for our first outing. Quit worrying about your weight; you don't need to. You don't have anything to worry about. Tall girls can always carry a few extra pounds. You're gorgeous just the way you are."

Julie was used to Brandon offering compliments, but gorgeous was never a word he had ever used in describing her before. 'What has gotten into him tonight?'

"Thank you, sir. But summer is coming and I won't be going to the beach cabin if I can't get into my bathing suit. I've been sitting at my desk for far too long.

Brandon sucked in his breath for a moment. Julie not coming to the lake with him would be horrible! Surely she was just joking. 'Ah, yes, writers and their exclamations over everything.'

Julie continued with no notice as to Brandon's surprise that she might not come to the cabin, "The new book is coming along now and I can send the next chapters to Richard for him to begin editing. I'll feel more confident after he sends me an edited portion. I know he likes it, but his written comments will make the rest of it go smoother. Then I'll have some time to get in a little exercise. The walking-trail a couple of blocks over from my place has been calling to me. 'Julie, get yourself over here, you, fat cow.' She chuckled and asked, "Are you still riding your bike to work every day?" Even though Julie had asked, she knew the answer. It didn't matter what the weather, he would be pedaling his way to the office. He had all the inclement weather gear he needed in his knapsack and nothing stopped him from his daily commute. She wished she could be as committed to exercise as Brandon was, but it just wasn't in her nature. She'd rather write and eat, neither of which were conducive to a slim figure.

They lingered a bit longer over dinner since the restaurant wasn't too busy. They knew that most of the theatre goers would probably come in after the play as they usually did as well. But since they had both been hungry, they decided to eat first. If they wanted a snack afterwards, they could go to DK's. Then Brandon remembered Julie had driven herself and met him there so that probably wouldn't happen. She would want to drive on home alone. 'Darn, why did I let her talk me into not picking her up.' He chided himself.

"Oh, look at the time, we'd best get to the theatre." Julie interrupted his thoughts. He looked at her blankly for a second, then said, "Right. Why don't you follow me to my office and I'll park in the garage there? I hope I still have a space. Since I've been riding my bike for several years, they may have reassigned it."

"That sounds like a good plan. No need for both of us to use the valet parking at the theatre. Then I can head for home after I drop you off." Just as Brandon had surmised. 'Darn,' he kicked himself again for agreeing to let her drive herself.

Their seats were in Row Five, Center Section, on the Aisle! 'Wow, Brandon's friend was good!' And so was the show. **Hamilton**, the award winning musical. Sixteen Tony award nominations and Eleven wins, *including* best musical. Julie had wanted to see it ever since it came out and she'd heard the reviewers raving about it. Julie didn't know if Brandon's friend's wife was a big theatre fan or not, but she certainly missed out seeing this one. Years from now she will be telling her grown baby how she missed seeing the hit show of the century because of him!

Brandon had looked over at Julie during the show and he could see the smile on her face and her head bobbing to the music. He was glad he could bring her to see it. Nothing made him happier than pleasing Julie. Julie had looked back at him and took his arm and gave it a little hug. During intermission, they went to the wine bar and had a glass. Julie said, "Just a small one please. I've got to drive home. I wonder if the rain has stopped?" Brandon kicked himself again for allowing her to drive herself to meet him. 'What was I thinking?'

After the show Julie gave Brandon a quick hug in the lobby as they waited for the valet to return with her car. She knew she was just dropping him off at this office building and heading for home and wanted him to know how much she had enjoyed herself this evening. She thanked him profusely again for the evening. The food, the conversation and the SHOW had been fantastic!

She pulled into the parking garage at Tetontian Romantics and as Brandon got out of the car, Julie waved and shouted "Bye Brandon, thanks again, love ya."

Brandon scoffed to himself with a shake of his head. She didn't realize just how much that phrase meant to him. If only she truly meant it. He had entertained the thought of telling Julie how he felt over dinner. The candlelight had been perfect and they had lingered over dessert and wine. It seemed like a romantic time to tell her that he loved her; that he'd loved her ever since high school. But he was afraid that telling her might end their long friendship. Going from friend to lover was a tricky step and he didn't want to jeopardize their friendship. He would be crushed if he proposed a stronger connection and she wanted to avoid it like the plague! But they weren't getting any younger. At thirty-four, they had both worked on their careers and let family life pass them by, but it wasn't too late. He desperately wanted a family and he wanted it to be with Julie!

CHAPTER 8

Eric hadn't talked to Julie for a couple of weeks. It wasn't that he didn't want to see the tall pretty blonde; it was just not the right time. He told himself that getting involved with a woman right now was not what he really needed. He wanted to keep details of the construction accident that had injured his dad a secret. He knew there was more to it than his dad had told him. He was sure that Streeter had cut corners and that's why the building had collapsed. What he didn't understand was why his dad wanted to cover it up to protect Streeter. Of course, they had been friends for many years, but that doesn't excuse the fact that people were injured and killed due to their negligence. Eric didn't really want to put the blame on his dad, but he wanted the truth to come out so that he could be vindicated. Yes, he had agreed to the settlement to protect George Folder and his company but losing his job and his license just didn't seem fair. If nothing else, he wanted his license back so he could again work as an architect; that was his life and it had been brutally taken away from him by his dad and Streeter!

Eric clenched his fists in anger and cried out to himself that he wanted revenge and he was going to get it no matter what the costs and any pretty little blonde who gets in his way would pay the price too. 'Damn, it dad, why wouldn't you listen to me? See, now I have to keep you in a coma until I decide what to do.'

He regretted telling Julie that he had been an architect and now he was concerned that he might have said too much. 'You know how nosy writers are', he said to himself. 'So best to stay away from her, so she doesn't ask more questions that I don't want to answer.'

He had seen her drive by in Stormy one evening when he was getting his mail. She had waved and he waved back. He half hoped she would stop, but it looked like she was going somewhere important all dressed up. He could see that she was wearing something blue which he knew would complement her dusty grey/blue eyes.

'There you go again, Eric Players, letting your interest in a pretty woman get in the way of your plans.' He had turned back to the house. Although it was a lovely house and suited his and his dad's needs, he felt trapped by the walls of the three-bedroom home and especially the steady hum of the machines from the last room down the hall. He wanted to have a normal life, but the decision he had made about his dad would keep him from that for now. In the few months since he'd moved there he had only gone out to the grocery store and to get other supplies. The neighborhood BBQ the ladies organized when they first moved in had been fun but he knew he couldn't develop any friendships with those families for fear they would find out about the accident. He couldn't go into details. Some of them had called afterwards with other invites, but he had politely declined and eventually they had stopped calling.

Now he had gone and spent the day car shopping with Julie and then cooking for her and he knew she was interested in him just as much as he was in her. The lie he had told to her about his dad having cancer was just the tip of the iceberg of lies he would have to tell her if they were to see each other on a regular basis. He knew she would ask again about his career as an architect. He would have to think of some plausible story. His mind was in a whirl and it was driving him crazy. He wanted to be with her again, but he knew he had to keep his secret.

Julie had told him about her early Journalism interest during high school and her first job after college and he feared her need to know details about him would be sparked if she knew much more, and that would not be beneficial to him. 'Once a Journalism Major, always a Journalism Major,' he told himself. 'Perhaps I could casually mention the construction accident of dad's and say that they had found cancer when he was in the hospital recuperating from that. Yes, that would work. At least that would clear up part of the lie. And when Dad passes, Julie will think it was from the cancer and not question the accident. Yes, that was a good start.' Eric went to fix a bite of supper content with his new plan to tell Julie about the accident, but nothing about his involvement as the building's architect. Tomorrow he would call her and ask her out. He smiled to himself. 'Yep, Eric, that's a good plan. You can see Julie and have a future with her.' He wasn't going to let his dad and the building accident get in the way of his life anymore.

Julie had been thinking about Eric too and wondering why he hadn't called. Their last *date* had gone well, or so she thought. He had spent the day cooking for her and the kiss on the forehead when she left was sweet and she had thought he was actually going to give her a real kiss twice that evening. When he had leaned over to help her take her sweater off when she got too warm in front of the fireplace, she anticipated that move to finish with a kiss. She had been ready and she thought he was too. The moment was something right out of one of her romance stories! Why he had backed away, she didn't know. Then at the front door, the kiss on the forehead could have been planted just a little lower! Her mind was swirling with wondering what he was feeling. She knew they enjoyed each other's company. Their car buying trip had been so much fun. The conversation had flowed easily on the two-hour drive. Eric seemed to enjoy the museum in spite of his saying museums were not his thing. Conversation had continued comfortably at DK's during supper afterwards. Whenever they were together, Julie felt an electric spark running between them. Surely, it wasn't just her feeling that way. She thought her instincts were good.

'So maybe he's just not that interested in a romantic involvement. He just needs a friend', she tried to tell herself. But she wanted more. The night she had driven to Fort Wayne to see **Hamilton** with Brandon, Eric had been getting his mail at the curb and she had honked and waved. His wave and smile certainly seemed like more than just a casual friend. She had the feeling that he would have liked her to stop and come in. Maybe she was reading too much into the look on his face, but she had felt a pull for it to be something more. She needed a reason to call him and then suddenly she thought she knew exactly what.

'I'm going to do it,' she decided. She picked up her phone and clicked on Eric's name in her contact list. A bit presumptuous of her to have added him maybe….

He answered on the second ring. "Julie, hi!" So, he had put her number in his contact list too. That says something. "Hi Eric. What's new? I haven't heard from you for a while. I hope everything is okay with your dad."

"Oh, yes, we're doing fine. I've been meaning to call you, but I've been busy. Dad is about the same. Nothing to report there. You?" Eric tried to keep his voice sounding casual.

Julie wondered what he was busy doing, but knew she had better not ask. Eric seemed glad that she called so best to leave that subject alone. "The new book is coming along swimmingly, to use one of my grandmother's sayings. I've sent a few more chapters off to the publisher. He's going to be doing a pre-edit of what I've done so far. I'm meeting with him later today. After I get his comments, I'll work on finishing it. I have most of the plot on paper notes and I will just need to tie it all together at the computer."

"That's great. I'm looking forward to reading it myself. Will I get to see a copy before it's published?"

"What? You're not willing to buy a copy? How am I supposed to become a best-selling author if I give it away?" Julie teased.

"Ooo, I hadn't thought of that. Of course, I will buy a copy. But I will want a signed one." Playing the game right back to her.

"You will have to come to the official book signing then. You know all authors have a book signing when they introduce their new book." Julie informed him.

"Oh dear, there's a lot to know about being friends with a writer. I need to learn the proper etiquette."

Julie laughed. She enjoyed their teasing banter. "Hey, before I forget why I called, would you feed my cat for me tomorrow? I'm going into Fort Wayne to meet with my publisher and I'm going to stay over if you would be willing to feed Spot."

There was a bit of silence on the line as Eric hesitated and Julie said, "Oh don't worry about it if you are busy. I usually take him with me. He loves to ride in the car unlike most cats. It's just that the hotel I stay in charges extra for pets. Never mind, I am imposing on you and our new friendship. Forget I called." She started to hang up when Eric said, "It's no bother. I didn't mean to hesitate. I was just thinking that maybe it would work better to bring Spot here. Would he do that? I don't mind at all, just wondering if he would be okay in a strange house."

"I'm sure he would be fine. He was a rescue kitten from the shelter. He was around a lot of different people all the time."

"Oh, sure. So, bring him over. What time you leaving?" Eric asked. He truly liked animals and Spot would be no bother.

"My meeting is at 4:00. Can I bring him by about 2:00?" Julie asked.

"Yep, that will work great. See you then." Later that day Julie rang Eric's bell with Spot in his travel carrier and a bag of his food in her arms.

"Come in Julie. Welcome Spot." Eric reached into the carrier for the cat and Spot let out a howl and scratched Eric on the arm as he leaped out of the carrier and dashed into the kitchen. Julie gasped in amazement, "Oh, I'm so sorry, Eric. He never reacts like that to strangers. He was fine the night you came to the cottage in the storm. Are you ok? Oh, boy, look at that scratch; we should put something on it. Oh, dear, I'm so sorry. I don't know what got into him." Julie was embarrassed that Spot had reacted that way. Cats can be so funny at times.

"Not to worry, Julie. I just scared him. He will be fine as soon as you are gone. I'm pretty good with animals. He just needs to get used to me and the house. You go to your meeting and don't worry about a thing." Eric assured her.

"Thank you so much, Eric. I will definitely need to fix you that roast and Yorkshire pudding sometime soon," Julie promised.

"I will hold you to that for sure." Eric said. "You can bring Spot anytime you want. We will be good buddies by the time you get home just wait and see."

Julie felt bad about leaving Spot with Eric and going off to Fort Wayne where she would meet Brandon for supper and a movie later after her meeting with Richard and the Board of Tetonkian Romantics. She wasn't in the habit of balancing two men at the same time, but Brandon was a dear friend and Eric was just a new acquaintance. It wasn't like she was dating both of them. Even if she did *want* to date Eric; the whole thing made her feel a bit guilty. She didn't want to betray her friendship with Brandon. She knew she should tell him about Eric. And she felt guilty about asking Eric to watch Spot. She realized her motive in that was to have another chance to see him. It was a strange and confusing time trying to juggle her life and the feelings she had for both of them.

The meeting with Richard and the Board went well. There were, of course, questions on when the new book would be finished. They were anxious to get it printed and in the market.

Julie assured them that it wouldn't be long. With Richard's pre-edit comments, she felt certain that she could be zipping out the last chapters by the end of May. The Board was pleased. The presses would just be finishing up a run of one of their other authors and the timing would be just right to put Julie's new book on right after.

Julie left the offices of Tetonkian Romantics with a satisfied smile on her face and took a cab to her hotel. There was a message at the front desk from Brandon. 'I will meet you in the hotel lobby at 6:30. We can get a quick bite before the movie at 8:00 then have dinner afterwards.' Julie thought that sounded great as long as she left room for the required popcorn at the movie. She wasn't too hungry yet; there had been sweet crescent rolls and coffee at the meeting and Julie had taken two. They were warm and drizzled with a buttery honey icing. She would have eaten three if she had thought she could get away without the Board thinking she was a starving writer! That wouldn't have been the best impression to leave at a meeting. She had noticed a look on one of the board member's face when she had taken her second one. But she enjoyed it anyway.

Brandon was waiting for her in the lobby at 6:30 as he said. Julie made sure she was on time as well, or at least close. She knew he was a stickler for punctuality. It was 6:35 as the elevator doors opened and she saw Brandon looking at this watch with a bit of frown on his face but it changed to a smile as he looked up and saw her getting off the elevator. She was dressed casually in tan slacks, green silk blouse and a cream colored jacket. Brandon watched as she crossed the lobby, her long slim legs gliding smoothly towards him. She was a stunning woman and he was always thrilled to spend time with her. He met her in the middle of the lobby and leaned down for a kiss on her cheek. She gave him a quick hug and said, "Sorry, I'm running a little late, we don't have to eat before the movie if you don't want to. I'm not starving and you know I will want popcorn at the theater. They were going to see **Green Book**, the academy award winning movie for best picture.

"That's fine with me; I had a late lunch at the office." Brandon responded. He was just happy to see her. He reached for Julie's hand at the curb as he opened the door of his car. Julie thought to herself, 'Brandon is such a great guy and such a catch for some lucky girl.' Their evening was relaxed and enjoyable as usual. The movie was excellent and they talked about it over hamburgers at a little bar around the corner from her hotel. It was well past midnight and Julie was feeling fatigued from her meeting at Tetonkian, the movie, and the late supper. Her eyes were getting droopy after the second beer and Brandon said, "Hey, sleepy girl, I'd better get you to your hotel before you fall asleep right here."

"Thanks, Brandon, it has been a busy day. You're right. I'm exhausted." She gave a big yawn and Brandon knew he had to get her back to the hotel. They walked with Brandon holding Julie's hand to be sure she didn't fall asleep right there on the sidewalk. "Hey, want to ride out to the lake with me on Saturday?" Brandon asked as he pushed the Up button on the hotel's elevator. "I've got some canned goods and staples to stock up for the season. Don't want to ruin our first weekend by running out of toilet paper or charcoal briquettes."

Julie laughed. "Yeh, that would not be fun, especially the briquettes." She teased him as she always did.

"I've got soap and shampoo, **TRESemme'**, the kind you like. Is there anything else specifically you want?" Brandon never failed to think about what she wanted or needed. 'What will I do without him in my life?' crossed her mind.

"Nope, sounds like you're prepared, as usual." Although she hadn't really heard what he said; she was so tired.

"So, around 2:00?" Brandon asked in anticipation.

Julie hesitated for a second. "As long as we don't stay too late. I've got to finish the new book. I promised Richard and the board, so I don't want to stay over."

"Oh, I wasn't planning on staying over. I just wanted to see if it's ready and stock in a few things. I paid Mrs. Deeringer to take care of it and her son is supposed to chop more wood. She was going to air out the cabin and wash all the curtains, towels and bedding. I know she always does a good job, but I like to check it over before we plan our first weekend.

I wish we could go down to the lake more often, but you know how things are at Tetonkian. It's been so busy. We have several new clients and Richard has given me more responsibility so I'm kind of hoping a promotion is in the picture." Brandon was eager to share this information with Julie. He was secretly hoping she would see him as a prosperous candidate for a future husband. "So 2:00 Saturday then?" He gave Julie a hug.

"Sure, see you then. Goodnight, love ya." Julie mumbled, barely awake enough to get to her room.

"Love you too." Brandon watched as the elevator door closed and Julie waved goodbye. He longed to tell her that he wanted their relationship to be more than just friends. She always said 'love ya' but he knew it was just a brotherly kind of love and he wished it could be more. He wondered where their relationship had gone wrong. He had hoped that after college their "friend" status would change, but it appeared as though that was just wishful thinking on his part.

As Julie pulled the covers up and snuggled into her pillow, her thoughts drifted to the two men in her life; one a long established friendship but no love interest and the other, only a new friend but definitely with potential. 'Hmmm, life is intriguing.' Julie slipped into a sound restful sleep.

On Saturday, Brandon arrived promptly at 2:00. He was driving his pickup truck. It was a standing joke between them because he called it his baby. His dad had found it when they were in high school and she had spent many a Saturday watching Brandon and his dad as they worked to restore it. It was a 1989 Dodge Shelby Dakota. It wasn't really vintage, since Ford leads in their F-series, but back in the day, Dodge wasn't all that backward either. Restoring it had taken a full summer. It had a 5.2 liter V8 engine that churned out 175 horsepower; the guys loved the way it sounded when they revved her up. Brandon had painted it a metallic blue and it shone as if stardust had been sprinkled over it to catch the sun reflecting the surface of the ocean. Seeing it brought back delightful memories of those summer days in the Jenkins' garage.

Brandon had make Julie their assistant, fetching tools, sodas, and sandwiches as they worked throughout the day. She enjoyed helping and watching the guys work. Besides, Brandon's dad had a radio in the garage tuned into his favorite oldies station. Rock 'n Roll blared out into the yard as they worked together. Julie had wondered why the neighbors hadn't complained, but the Jenkins family were well known and respected, so if Harry Jenkins wanted to boogie on Saturday afternoons in his garage, no one really cared.

Julie remembered how crushed Brandon had been when Harry had died suddenly at 72. He was still working part time at the **Walmart Super Center** and it had been a huge shock when he had come home in the middle of his shift not feeling well. It was not like Harry at all to leave work early. Brandon's sister, Carolyn, had taken him to Monique's community hospital and they said he had suffered a mild heart attack and transferred him by ambulance to Fort Wayne's Intensive Care Unit. When Brandon had gone to see him that evening, his dad was looking good and wanted his razor and toothbrush brought the next day and Brandon had said he would get them. A few hours later after Brandon had gone home, Carolyn phoned and said the hospital had called saying when Harry had tried to get out of bed to go to the bathroom, his heart had literally burst and he was gone instantly. Brandon couldn't imagine the vibrant dad he had spent so many hours laughing and working with could be gone. So now, the truck they had restored together was a treasured memory of that time. Julie loved riding in it with Brandon seeing the joy it brought him remembering his dad.

Brandon met her at the door as she was coming out. "I see you got Old Blue out of storage for the summer. A bit early, isn't it? Julie asked. "What would your dad say?'

"Well, it's a beautiful day and Old Blue needs her pipes cleared out and he would approve." Brandon answered excitedly. "Come on, hop in. I have everything in the back. I told Mrs. Deeringer I would call her by 3:00 if there was anything else that needed to be done. She said she had to be at her sister's by 4:00, so we've got to get going so we don't hold her up. You know how she gets grumpy if her plans get changed. And I don't want to talk to her if she's in one of her grumpy moods." I know she'll have taken care of everything as usual so I'm not too worried.

"You're so right about her getting grumpy", Julie said. "Remember that time she forgot to take the quilts to the cleaners? I thought she was going to bite your head off when you reminded her about them."

"Yeah, and I wasn't mad. I just asked her about them and she flew into a rage about how busy she was taking care of her invalid sister and how lazy her boy, Jerrod, was and that was the reason she hadn't gotten around to getting the quilts to the cleaners." Brandon felt sorry for the middle aged widow who had to deal with the problems of her dysfunctional family. He made a mental note to compliment her on the cabin and put an extra $20 in her pay envelope.

"I'm sure she has done her usual good job." Julie said and Brandon agreed.

"Hey, aren't you bringing Spot along? He always enjoys the woods around the cabin," Brandon asked. He and Spot were good friends.

"No, not today. I haven't cleaned his travel carrier out since the last time I had him out. I hope he won't be mad. Don't tell him." Julie hoped Brandon wouldn't ask when and where she had taken Spot out.

Brandon laughed. "You and that cat. You act like he's human."

"Well, he is my best buddy." Julie pouted.

"I thought I was your best buddy." Brandon feigned a hurt look. Julie gave his arm a smack as she got in the truck.

It was only a quick half hour to Lake Ferrell. As they entered the lane to their driveway for the long drive down to the cabin, Julie noticed the bluebells were blooming in the woods. She shouted, "Stop!" Brandon slammed on the brakes. "What? Did I hit something?" Frightened by whatever Julie had seen.

"No, I just wanted to stop and pick some bluebells." Julie laughed.

"Oh, and for bluebells, we shout *stop* at the top of our lungs like a madman!" Brandon exclaimed. "A madwoman, sir," Julie said. "Sorry, I just was excited to see them. I remember my great Uncle Louis in England used to take me when I was a kid to go pick them. He would fetch me on his scooter and I would hang on for dear life as he dodged in and out of traffic. I thought for sure we would be killed; I was always so glad to get out of town into the countryside." The memory had popped into Julie's head when she had seen the bluebells in the woods.

"You've talked about your Uncle Louis before. He must have been fun to be around when you were a kid." Brandon asked hoping she would share more.

"Yes, but he was a bit odd. I think he might have been gay. But, of course, no one talked about things like that in the 50s, especially in England. And I was too young to know anything about it. He was just my great uncle who always took me to do things whenever we were there. I think I might have been his favorite great niece. I remember him taking me to the school where he taught when I was about six. I was terrified. He sat me down on a chair in the back of the room while he was at the front of the class. I was scared being left back there all alone. I didn't know anyone but him and no one spoke to me at first and when they did I couldn't understand their accents. It was really a strange thing for a six-year old. When lunchtime came around, he took me to the lunchroom and sat me down all alone again while he went off to do whatever he needed to do, and I started to cry. I'll always remember they were serving beans on toast and I didn't like them. When he came back and saw me crying, he told me there was no need to cry. I didn't have to eat the beans, but that there wasn't anything else for lunch. The decision was mine, eat them or go hungry. I tried to eat them, then I cried again and also wet my pants. It was not a good day. And I *still* don't like beans on toast."

"Was Uncle Louis mad?" Brandon asked with concern.

"No, I don't think so. I was little, you know, and in a strange country. He just said we had to go home and that was it. Since he had never married, I don't think he really knew what to do with a six-year old. His students were older, but he always wanted me to come visit when we were in England. For many years I wrote him letters. He always wrote back and as an adult I continued to visit him until he died. He was a special part of my British family life.

"Sounds like a really sweet guy." Brandon smiled at her.

"Yes, I was very fond of him. He was always my favorite uncle. And the bluebells brought back a rush of memories. Sorry about my shouting stop. That was stupid of me; I could have caused an accident."

"No, problem. We are stopped now and all is well. Let's go get some bluebells." Brandon climbed down from his seat and walked around to open Julie's door.

When they arrived at the cabin, of course it *was* clean and tidy just as they had anticipated. Mrs. Deeringer had washed everything and scrubbed the hardwood floors till they glowed before she put down the clean rugs. The beds were made up and she had opened the windows to air out the stale winter air. Brandon called her to say everything was spic and span. He said he would leave her pay envelope on the kitchen table and she could stop by any time to get it.

Julie found a large drinking glass to use as a vase and she arranged the bluebells in it and placed it in the center of the kitchen table. After looking over the cabin and calling Mrs. Deeringer, Brandon said, "Help me bring in the supplies? I've got a picnic lunch packed and we can eat on the front porch before we head back." Julie hadn't expected a picnic, but she should have known that Brandon would think of it and have it all ready. It was 3:45 by the time they got everything unloaded from Old Blue and Julie was a bit concerned about getting back to Monique; but she didn't want to disappoint Brandon. "Can I get things out of the picnic basket and set the table while you finish up?" she asked.

"Sure, go ahead. There's not much. Just some sandwiches and chips. I tossed in a package of **Oreos** too. We don't have time to build a fire and make s'mores, so the **Oreos** will have to do. I put some cold beers and soda in the frig just now."

"Do you want a beer or a soda?" Julie called to him as he was getting the last of the boxes unpacked in the kitchen.

"Better have a soda, I guess. I'm driving. I know one beer wouldn't hurt, but no sense in taking a chance of getting stopped and the officer smelling beer on my breath." Brandon was always the logical, conservative one and Julie wondered why she had even asked. She should have known he would only drink a soda today. She opted for a beer though; she wasn't driving and a cold beer sounded good.

"Picnic is ready then. Come and get it." When Julie opened the basket, she chuckled. Brandon had made his favorite sandwich, peanut butter, bologna and dill pickles. He had loved them since he was a kid. Julie had said "ewww" when he first brought them for lunch back in high school. They were sitting at the lunchroom table when he had urged her to just try one bite. She had hesitated and gingerly put the end of the sandwich in her mouth. After she had a bit into it, she was afraid to chew. Brandon had laughed at her and said, "chew it up, you silly". When she did, she was sold! Who knew? Peanut, bologna and dill pickles? Sounds like a horrible combination, but the taste of the three ingredients together was awesome.

She unwrapped the sandwiches and opened the bag of chips and the **Oreos**. She laid out the paper plates and napkins while Brandon finished stocking the cupboards. He wasn't long and joined her on the front porch and they sat in his green Adirondack chairs as they ate and listened to the birds singing in the treetops. There was no need for conversation; it was so lovely and peaceful. There were squirrels frolicking around the yard doing a mating dance. Watching them, Julie felt sad that it might all come to an end, if she and Eric became an item.

CHAPTER 9

On the drive home, Brandon asked, "What ya doin' next Sunday? We could spend the day at the cabin if you are finished with the new book by then."

"Oh, that would have been lovely, but one of my neighbors invited me for dinner." She hated lying to Brandon, but we she wasn't ready to tell him about Eric. She knew he wouldn't understand why *she* was going to do the inviting and would be cooking for another man. He probably would be hurt and she didn't want to ruin their friendship, but she wasn't ready to go into detail about her feelings for Eric, so it was best to be vague.

"Sounds nice, I'm glad you've found friends in the neighborhood. It's probably a bit lonely at the end of a cul-de-sac like that. Spot isn't much of a conversationalist, huh? I wish I wasn't in Fort Wayne; we could get together more often." He didn't ask anything else and Julie was happy to let that particular bit of conversation come to an end. When Brandon dropped her off, she gave him a quick hug and scurried away with a wave and a "love ya".

She was anxious to call Eric, but she waited til the beginning of the week to gather her thoughts. She was pleased when he seemed as eager as her when she said, "I'm calling to invite you to dinner this coming Sunday night. I believe I bragged about my roast and Yorkshire pudding cooking abilities."

"Yes, you did and I have been wondering why I haven't been invited to partake."

"So, does Sunday night work for you?"

"Uhmm". There was a pause and Julie's heart skipped a beat. "It does if you're willing to come cook here. You know, my dad and all..."

"Oh, of course, I wasn't thinking. I'm sorry." Julie said with relief.

"That's okay. I could get the home caregiver if you would prefer to be in your own kitchen."

"Oh, no, your kitchen is fine as long as you don't mind the mess. I'm a sloppy cook. You will have to hire a *Maid for a Day* after I'm done."

"Don't you remember the kitchen after I was done cooking the Spaghetti Bolognese. Yorkshire pudding cannot be that messy. I think I've got all the necessary appliances and pots and pans. Do you need anything special?"

"Nope. Stormy and I will head to the grocery store to get everything. And, of course, I'm going to park at the far end of the lot to avoid any reckless hit and run drivers!"

"Good idea. What time you coming Sunday?"

"Well, depends on what time you want to eat. Six-ish for the meal?"

"Sounds good."

"Ok, then, I will need about four hours for the roast. Is that too long to put up with me messing up your kitchen?"

"I can't think of anyone else I would prefer to get messy with."

"Oh, does that mean you will be helping? I could use a sous-chef."

"Ahhh, probably not; I won't be much help, but I can open the bottle of wine. What goes best with roast and Yorkshire pudding?"

"Well, a red Bordeaux works nicely or a beer too. A traditional ale or porter is usually an under estimated match with roast beef, my grandmother insisted. A British classic ale like Timothy Taylor's Landlord would be good. If you are worried about the extra carbs in the Yorkshire, then beer is the logical choice." Julie was happy to share her knowledge of British cuisine.

"You know your stuff with this English cooking. I'm not worried about the carbs, but that Timothy Taylor sounds good. Will I find it in our grocery store or should I drive to Fort Wayne to the liquor store?"

"Oh, don't worry about it. I have some in my pantry. I'll bring it." She was prepared to make the evening as special as possible.

"Isn't there something I can do?"

"Sit at the counter and keep me company. You can tell me about your career as an architect."

Eric knew it! He just knew it! She wanted more information. "Former career, remember. There's not much to tell, but I will share the boring details if you like." Eric wanted to kick himself. 'Oh, crap, why did I say that!'

"I don't think it will be boring. My cooking and talking endlessly about my new book and my illustrious writing career will be what's boring." Julie joked.

"You don't know what boring is. I guarantee my defunct career will win." Eric hoped she would let it go.

"Okay, the competition is on. You put together your best stories on architecture and I will tell you all about the new book 'til you beg for mercy. See you Sunday around 1:30." Julie clicked the red dot and a warm rush came over her. She did like Eric Players and it seemed as if he liked her too.

At the same time, Eric was sitting at the kitchen counter with his head in his hands thinking, 'Oh boy, now I've done it. An afternoon and evening of me talking about my failed architectural career. Better work on a good story. Or maybe I should tell her the truth, well at least part of it. What could that hurt?'

Later Julie was relaxing on the living room couch making a grocery list for Sunday's meal. 'I can do small whole potatoes with the skins on. They would be good with a mint sauce. What to do for a veggie? I wonder if Eric likes roasted Brussel sprouts? They're Brandon's favorite. Oh, here I go again. Now why did Brandon pop into my head when I'm anticipating a date with Eric? Darn, it's just we've known each other for so long and shared a lot of meals together, I guess. It's going to be hard to tell him I've fallen for someone else. I hope he'll understand. He's always wanted what's best for me. But it will be hard not seeing him. I'll miss our summer weekends at the beach cabin.' Another thought popped into her head, 'Maybe Eric has a friend we could introduce to Brandon. If they hit it off, we could still be close and the four of us could go to the beach cabin together.' It was a thought anyway. Suddenly she realized how much she'd miss the cabin and Brandon's friendship and then suddenly the thought of him romantically involved with another woman made her feel a little jealous.

On Friday, Julie went to the store with her list. She had decided on the potatoes around the roast for sure and the Brussels. A peach flan would make a lite dessert after the heavy meal. They could have it later with a glass of wine. A light dessert wine like Riesling would go well with the flan. She had been surprised to see it in the grocery store on an earlier shopping trip and she hoped they still had today. She had all the other ingredients for the gravy and the Yorkshire and Eric said he had the necessary utensils. She drove off to the store with a smile on her face. She was anticipating a wonderful Sunday getting to know Eric better. 'Maybe that elusive kiss would be in the making after dinner as we are sipping our wine in the living room close to the fireplace.' She was writing the scene in her mind.

Eric was anticipating Sunday too with a little apprehension. He, of course, was looking forward to seeing Julie and sharing a meal with her, just not talking about his career. The Yorkshire sounded good and he was anxious to try it, but he was not so anxious for the topic of conversation. 'I'll get her talking about her new book and maybe she'll forget about my architecture career. Oh, yeh, right, fat chance of that! She was a former journalist for a big newspaper; she wouldn't forget. Okay, maybe writing the obits wasn't really a journalist, but she did major in Journalism in college. It's in her blood even if she isn't beating the pavement for a story, you dummy.' Eric berated himself and worried about it all week. He had decided to tell part of the story. He made up his mind that he could pull off being a bit vague on details. Maybe that would satisfy her.

Julie was out of bed early Sunday morning. Yes, she knew she didn't need to be at Eric's until 1:30 to start cooking, but she wanted to shower and fix her hair and makeup to perfection. And she knew it would take her awhile to decide on what to wear. Spot had sat on the end of the bed watching her curiously as she tried on different outfits. This was supposed to be a casual evening, she reminded herself and she was going to be cooking and she again reminded herself how messy she could be in the kitchen when preparing a big meal. So, finally she decided on jeans and her white satin blouse with the quarter length sleeves. It was a risk to wear it for cooking, but she wanted to look nice even if she was going for a casual look. She wouldn't have to roll up sleeves to avoid getting anything on the cuffs. Lastly, she chose one of her mom's favorite aprons to throw on top for safety; that was a must. She could take it off when she was ready to serve and put on the green cashmere sweater vest that highlighted her eyes and gave them a bit of an emerald glow. It was light enough for a spring evening. She hoped she had made the right choice and that Eric would be casual as well.

Finally, with her attire decided, she turned to packing the supplies in a large plastic tub that she could easily carry up the street. She had made a list of everything she needed. It would have been simpler to cook in her own kitchen, but she understood why Eric wanted to stay in his house to be near his dad. He probably had flour, but she packed the small one pound bag she had purchased just in case. He said he didn't cook much so maybe he didn't have any on hand. But, then again, he had made the pasta. So he must have eggs and flour and milk. But, then again, it was easier just to take it all. She was driving herself crazy thinking about it! She didn't want to make him feel bad if he didn't have everything she needed. She wanted this afternoon to go smoothly. She wanted the opportunity to visit with him about his architectural career and worrying about all the necessary ingredients for supper would make them both tense. She was a little disturbed with herself for offering to cook such an elaborate meal. A Sunday roast with potatoes and Yorkshire and gravy and Brussels! What had she been thinking? And an English peach flan for dessert! She must be losing her mind!

'Ok, calm down, girl. You've got this. A hot shower is the answer. Everything is packed ready to go, so go take a long relaxing shower.' Julie headed to the bathroom anticipating the afternoon and evening with Eric.

A couple of hours later she didn't know why she had been so nervous; the cooking was going well and so was their afternoon. Eric proved to be an excellent sous chef. He remained in the kitchen the entire time and peeled and cut up the Brussels. He whipped the egg, milk and flour for the Yorkshire and opened the can of peach slices for the flan. Julie had decided not to make the flan from scratch. She had purchased the cake and the can of peaches instead to save herself the hassle, but she did make the glaze topping to pour over the top. She showed Eric how to arrange the slices evenly around the edge of the cake, making the circles smaller as you approached the center. Eric then poured the glaze and the dessert was ready. It looked perfect and she put in it his refrigerator for later.

Eric had set the table in the dining room with a lovely tablecloth and candles. He had decided he wanted to try the Timothy Taylor's Landlord ale with the meal and Julie had purchased the sweet Reisling wine to go with dessert. They had worked well together. Much like she and Brandon did when they were in the kitchen.

'There I go again thinking about Brandon when I'm with Eric.' Julie chided herself. She and Eric hadn't talked much during meal prep other than instructions on the cooking and family recipes. He had shared more information about his Italian grandmother and Julie had talked about her British family. Julie loved hearing about his life and sharing her own.

As they sat down at the dining room table she turned to Eric and said, "Tell me more about your architectural career."

'Yep, there it is. Ms. Journalism at work.' Eric thought. "There is actually not much to tell." Eric started slowly thinking about how to relate the information he had decided to share. "I worked for a large firm in Philadelphia, but left to take care of dad. I don't mean to sound like I'm bragging, but I don't work now because I earned quite a lot when I was working and made some good investments. I sold my high rise condo in downtown Philadelphia and rented out my dad's house in Middetown and we came here and bought this place. There's not much else. I've lived a pretty boring life compared to yours."

"Mine? What's so exciting about mine?" Julie wondered why he thought her life was more interesting than his.

"Journalism Major, obituary columnist, romance novelist, Red Hot Mama driver." Eric teased, hoping to get her talking about herself and her career.

Julie laughed, "Yep, that sounds like me. Very exciting. But you left out teacher."

"Teacher? You never mentioned teacher. You were a teacher? When?"

"After I left the **Journal Gazette** in Fort Wayne. I was just thinking about starting my writing career and knew that I needed a job to live. Beginning writers don't make much, you know."

"I'm sure it does take a while to get established unless you're **J.K. Rowling**. Well, what did you teach?" Eric asked, drawing Julie out.

"Wait a minute, you know **J.K. Rowling's** work? Don't tell me you are a **Harry Potter** fan? I would never have guessed in a million years!"

"Why? I like a little fantasy to spice up my otherwise boring life. Forget about that and tell me about your teaching career."

"I had Minored in English Lit in College so I brushed up on things and got my teaching certificate and taught Third Grade English/Social Studies, that's all."

"Well, I'll be. You never cease to amaze me, Julie Avery. A teacher, huh?"

"Yep, those third graders are so cute. I loved it. I would write in the evenings and submit my stories to publishers. When I finally sold a few, I knew that I wanted to write full time so I resigned. I still sub occasionally and I have one girl I'm tutoring at home. I go to her house one day a week. I manage to bring in a little to live on while my writing career is taking off. I can tap into my savings if I need to, but I did get a nice advance on the new book from Tetonkian Romantics, so that helps."

Eric was pleased that Julie had seemed to forget about his architectural career. He wanted to keep her talking. "A tutor?

I never would have guessed. Is that where you were going yesterday? I saw someone pick you up in a blue truck."

"Oh, no that was my high school friend, Brandon. We were going to his beach cabin to get it ready for the season." Julie was a little hesitant to say much more about Brandon. She didn't want Eric to think that they had a relationship other than friends.

"Beach cabin? Where is there a beach around here?" Eric urged her to go on.

"It's not really a beach cabin in the true sense of the word. It's a log cabin in the woods about a half hour south of here on Lake Ferrell. But Brandon did make a sandy beach along the edge of the lake so I call it our beach cabin," Julie explained.

"*Our* beach cabin? Sounds like you and this Brandon are close," Eric questioned prying to keep her talking.

"Yes, we are but not romantically if that's what you mean. We've been friends forever."

"Friends with benefits?" Eric asked. It came out before he could catch himself and he was instantly sorry, because the look on Julie's face changed immediately.

Julie was a little offended at that suggestion. "That's really none of your business, but *No*. Just friends, long term and very good friends."

"Oooh, sorry. A sore subject?" Eric tried to tease her, but he could see that she hadn't liked his comment about Brandon.

"No, but I think my friendship with Brandon is just that and nothing for us to discuss." Julie decided to change the subject before Eric asked any other questions, so she again approached the subject of Eric's dad's cancer. "How is your dad doing with the cancer treatments?"

"Oh, he's not doing treatments. No need. It was too far advanced." Eric knew he was getting himself in deeper with the lie but he had to say something now that she had tossed the ball back into his court. He wanted to get Julie off the subject of his dad but wasn't sure how; they definitely couldn't talk about her *friend* Brandon; she had made that abundantly clear. "When dad had a construction accident, they found a tumor during the X-rays and removed it, but there wasn't much else they could do. I should have told you that before, but I just didn't want to go into details about his injuries."

"So your dad was in an accident?" Julie was really intrigued now.

Eric felt a rise of panic. She was going to keep on with the questions. "Yes, he has been a contractor all his life and he's been the manager on a lot of projects. There was an accident on his last job site and he was injured quite badly. The doctors have put him in a medically induced coma so he will be without pain while he heals. I'm sorry I didn't just tell you that in the first place, but it was easier to tell you about the cancer and let it go at that. Forgive me?" Eric didn't want his *confession* to ruin their evening and he hoped Julie would actually let it go at that.

"Gosh, Eric, I'm so sorry. No problem, I understand. It must be hard taking care of him like that." Julie was genuinely concerned for Eric's dad.

"Well, not really. The taking care of him is easy. The machines are doing all the work. I just bathe him and keep his bed changed, catheter emptied, you know."

"I know, but I meant seeing him like that in the coma. Were you and your dad close?"

Before he realized it Eric found himself saying, "Oh, yes, we worked together on a lot of projects." When it came out of his mouth, he knew he had blundered. There was no recovery at this point.

"Oh, were you the architect and your dad the project manager?" Julie was getting a picture now of the status of their relationship.

"Yes, and when he was injured on my project, I didn't want to work anymore without him." Eric hoped that his answer would suffice and Julie would drop the issue.

"That must have been terrible. Was this in Philadelphia?"

"Yes, and I am glad to be away from there." Eric desperately wanted to get away from this topic of conversation. "Julie, this meal has been wonderful. You out did yourself. And the Yorkshire pudding was fabulous. But why do they call it pudding? It's more like a bread, isn't it?" He hoped he could get her back to talking about herself.

"Actually, it is kind of like a pudding, with the eggs, milk and flour. If you added sugar and cinnamon before it's baked, it would be a popover for dessert. And the British call any dessert a pudding. But, you should eat a Yorkshire pudding only with the gravy over it. And traditionally, it is served *before* the rest of the meal. It's only become this aberration of eating it along with the roast and potatoes and veg as times have changed. It would be kind of an appetizer. The true posh British person would only have it with the gravy or perhaps with sausages baked in the middle and they call that *toad-in-the-hole*."

"Wow, a true British lesson along with the meal. I love it." Eric declared.

Julie laughed and added, "And only with roast beef. Some restaurants refuse to serve it with roast chicken, but people nowadays serve it however they want. I found that I prefer it with my meat and veg instead of first and I like it with chicken as well."

"Yes, I think I would too." They continued talking about the meal and British customs and Eric felt like Julie had forgotten the subject of his dad's accident and Eric's career. He thought he had maneuvered through it nicely and hoped that it would be the end of it. He certainly didn't want to go into the lawsuit proceedings and his having to take the responsibility as the architect. She didn't need to know those details. "Hey, let's go to the living room and have dessert." He suggested.

"Are you ready for dessert? I'm stuffed. Later for me. Let's clear the table and get these dishes washed. Since I've made my usual mess in the kitchen; it will take a while to clean up. Maybe then I can find a bit of room for the flan." Julie got up from the dining room table and started clearing the dishes.

"You don't have to clean my kitchen. I will do that tomorrow." Eric stated.

"I insist. My mother taught me to help with the dishes whenever I am a guest for a meal at someone's house." And I always do what my mother says, Julie joked.

"But you were the cook. That's different." Eric reminded her.

"In *your* kitchen." Julie insisted as she reached for her apron again. "Come on, this won't take long and it will be all done. It will give us a bit of time to digest that big meal before we relax by the fire with our flan and wine. Deal?"

"Never could change a woman's mind once it's made up. No more argument from me. Just as long as we get dessert. I want to try that flan I made." Eric teased.

"You made? I think we owe that to **Sara Lee**." Julie reminded him.

"Yes, she helped, but I put the peaches on top. I arranged them just perfectly." Eric put his shoulders back and boasted theatrically.

"Yes, you did." They bantered back and forth as they cleared the table and loaded the dishwasher. It didn't take long to get the kitchen counters wiped down and everything back in place. "I'm ready for a glass of wine in front of the fireplace, if you are." Julie was anticipating a kiss at some point this evening and the thought of it sent a tingle down her back.

"Absolutely. I will get the fire going after I check on dad. You bring the wine and the glasses. I'll be right back."

Julie actually wanted to go with him to see his dad, but Eric hadn't invited her and she felt awkward in suggesting it. Maybe another time, she decided. The wine glasses were in the cabinet in the dining room and Julie got them. She decided to include a couple of napkins and she opened the drawer below the glass doors of the cabinet.

As she pulled it open, she realized the napkins were not in those drawers. It was full of papers and she glanced at the top one and read, *Streeter Construction vs Folder Architecture in the District Court of the State of Pennsylvania in and for the City and County of Philadelphia*. She didn't have time to read any further as she heard Eric coming down the hall. She remembered how upset he had seemed when she had casually looked into the open door of his bedroom. She knew he would be much more disturbed if he thought she was snooping through his personal papers. She closed the drawer quietly and opened the cabinet and got out two wine glasses.

"Dad is sleeping peacefully," Eric said as he joined her in the dining room. "I hope he is having pleasant dreams. Do you supposed people dream when they are in a medically induced coma?"

"Gosh, I don't know. I've never been around anyone in a medically induced coma. Does he look like he's dreaming, you know, the REM sleep? They say when someone is having a dream, they have the rapid eye movement. Do you think I could see your dad sometime?" Julie asked hesitantly.

Eric thought, 'She's never going to let up about it,' so he said. "Ok, come on, let's go down there. He won't know you are there, but you can look in on him. I do it several times a day. As long as the machines are working and I empty the catheter, there's not much else anyone can do.

"Do you talk to him? They say people in a coma can hear you."

"I talk to him when I give him a bath every morning and make sure he isn't getting any bed sores. But I don't think a medically induced coma is the same."

"I really don't know either, but it couldn't hurt." Julie walked into the bedroom and was shocked by all the equipment and the big man lying in the bed. "Oh, my." She approached the bedside and leaned over, "Hi Mr. Players, I'm Julie Avery. I'm your neighbor. I live in the little cottage down the lane at the end of the cul-de-sac. I know your son, Eric. He's a wonderful guy to be taking such good care of you. I hope we will get to meet in person when you are better. God Bless." Julie turned away and Eric saw that she had tears in her eyes; those sparkling blue/grey eyes a man could get lost in.

As they walked back up the hallway to the living room, Eric put his arm around Julie's shoulder. Julie leaned over and put her head next to him. "I don't know how you do it. It must be heart breaking for you to see him like that."

Eric wasn't sure what to say right then. She was tucked under his arm and he felt like a mother Robin protecting her young. His emotions were all in a tangle. He knew he was falling for Julie and he knew he shouldn't. 'You don't need this complication, stupid. Get this woman out of your life now!' The words were so clear in his head, he wasn't sure if he hadn't actually said them aloud.

They walked slowly into the living room and as Julie started to pull away, Eric turned her body towards him and took her into his arms and lightly touched her lips with his. He immediately felt Julie's response as she arched her back closer to him. His arms tightened and hers slid up around his neck as the soft kiss began to smolder into something more intense. Her lips tasted like peaches and cream, even though they hadn't yet partaken of the flan. He couldn't get enough of her. His hands wanted to touch her body everywhere and he softly ran them up and down her back and gently squeezed her thigh. He could feel her breath increasing and he wanted to sweep her up and carry her to his bed.

'STOP, you idiot', rang out in his head. What are you doing?' And just as quickly as it had started, it ended. Eric released Julie and apologized. "Oh, Julie, I am so sorry. It's been a long time since I've enjoyed being with a woman and I got carried away in the moment."

Breathlessly Julie exclaimed. "Eric, I've been wanting you to do that for days. You didn't have to stop." She almost pleaded with him, wanting more.

"I didn't mean for it to go this far. You have been a wonderful friend. I loved the meal tonight and you were so sweet to go see dad. I can't apologize enough for my behavior. Please forgive me." He turned away from her for a moment and when he turned back his demeanor had changed. "You probably should go now."

"What?" Julie was dumbfounded. 'What just happened?' Eric practically ushered her to the door physically. His arm was on her back, the same arm and hands that had been caressing her just seconds ago, were now pushing her out the front door. "I'll call you later."

Tears came to Julie's eyes as she stood there on his doorstep looking at the closed door behind her pondering the last few minutes. 'What in the world was that all about?' She knew he wanted that kiss as much as she did and more. She had felt his arousal and his breath had increased as much as hers. His hands felt like fire when they slid down her thigh and cupped her buttocks. She had wanted him to scoop her up and never stop 'til they were lying on his bed naked entwined with each other. And yet, there she stood, cast out like a stranger. She looked down the street to see if the cops were coming, she felt like she was a burglar he had just caught and forced out of his house! Julie walked down the street to her cottage shaking her head in disbelief. She was almost too surprised and mad to cry.

Sleep didn't come easy that night. Julie tossed and turned, she couldn't help going over and over in her mind the evening's progression. They had enjoyed cooking dinner together. Eric had said so. Check. They were going to have the peach flan with the dessert wine in the living room near the glow of the fireplace. Check. Everything going well so far. Eric had said he wanted to look in on his dad and she had asked to go along. No hesitation on his part there. Check. She had talked to Mr. Players. Check. They had walked up the hallway and he had put his arm around her and she had snuggled closer. Check, check, check. Then, the kiss! Thinking about it again, made her heart start pumping faster. She could hear the rapid thump, thump, thump in her ears. The kiss! 'Oh, my gosh. I was on fire and he was too. I know it! But what happened for him to pull away so abruptly and toss me out like an old shoe?' There was no answer forthcoming at the moment.

The next morning Julie wanted to call Eric, but she didn't know where to even start the conversation. Should she be casual and apologetic or hurt and demand to know what happened? She was starting to get angry thinking about it. He had treated her like a streetwalker, escorting her out when he was finished with her. 'Thank goodness, we didn't make it to the bedroom. He would have turned into a monster for sure.' Julie's anger made up her mind. "Eric Players, you can go to Hell!" she said out loud.

Julie plodded down the hallway in her pink fuzzy slippers and robe with a cup of Earl Grey and sat down at her computer. She scanned the last few pages of the new book and then just sat there staring at it. Her heart certainly wasn't into writing a romance novel at the moment. Her thoughts drifted to, 'What had Eric talked about last night when they had been sharing their careers?' She opened Google and typed in *Philadelphia Architectural firms*.

A long list popped up and Julie scanned down through them. One had a link to a news story attached and Julie clicked on it. *BUILDING DESIGNED BY FOLDER ARCHITECTURE COLLAPSES*, the headline read. Julie read the article with her heart pumping wildly. *A thirty-five story high rise apartment building known as Capitol Avenue Apartments collapsed downtown today. At first report, Streeter Construction, the contractor for the job, denied any allegations of faulty materials and placed the blame on the designer, Folder Architecture. Several workers were injured with some believed to have been killed. No further information is available at this time as lawyers for both companies meet.*

She Googled for more articles, but didn't find anything else. 'That was it?! No other information? So this is why Mr. Eric Players doesn't want to talk about his career or his dad's accident. His dad must have worked for Streeter Construction and Eric worked for Folder Architecture and designed the building. The puzzle is all coming together now. I wonder how I can find out more? Brandon! He has a friend who is a police detective! I'll bet he can find the information.' Julie grabbed the phone and clicked on Brandon's office number in her contact list.

Brandon answered on the third ring. "Julie, what are you doing calling me at the office on a Monday morning? Is everything alright?"

Julie smiled to herself, bless her friend, Brandon, always concerned about her. "Brandon, would it be possible for you to find out some information through your friend, the police detective. What's his name, Don Graverton?"

"Yes, well, maybe. What's up? Why do you need the police? What's happened?" Brandon's voice was getting that high pitched sound as it did whenever he was worried or thought she might be in trouble.

"Calm down, Brandon," Julie assured him. "Nothing's happened to me. I just need some information about a construction accident that happened in Philadelphia last year."

"Construction accident? What are you talking about? Julie, I have to go right now, George is on the intercom. We've got a meeting in a few minutes. Can I call you back?"

Julie sighed. She wanted to tell Brandon all about Eric and the information she had just found out and she hoped he would be willing to contact his friend to scout out more. Brandon usually liked a good mystery and often told Julie she should write one. 'Well, maybe this could be the start of it,' Julie thought. 'But I can't do anything until I have more information. You'd better call back quickly, Brandon Jenkins.' Julie would be impatiently waiting by the phone until he did.

CHAPTER 10

When Brandon finally called back, Julie filled him in on what she knew about Eric Players, Folder Architecture, Streeter Construction and the accident on the job site at the Capitol Avenue Apartments building in Philadelphia.

"That's awful. How do you know all this?" Brandon asked.

"Remember that neighbor I told you about where I was going for supper? Well, that's him. We've been friends for a few weeks. He's been taking care of his dad who was injured in an accident and I was concerned about them and then Eric helped me find Stormy after Red Hot Mama was destroyed." Julie knew Brandon was probably going to be upset with this news, but it needed to be told if she wanted his help. She was right.

"What? He helped you buy your new car?" Brandon's voice began to rise again to that high pitched sound. He was getting upset.

"Yes, he was there at the grocery store when the accident happened and he offered to help. It was a thank you for me helping him during that awful thunderstorm we had a several weeks ago." Julie had a bit of explaining to do to make Brandon understand.

"The storm? I don't know what you're talking about. How did you help him?" Brandon asked with more than concern in his voice. He didn't like where this conversation was going.

Oh, boy. Julie knew she should have told Brandon about meeting Eric earlier, but she hadn't and now she had some explaining to do. "His power went out that morning and he came to my place to ask if he could use the phone. I woke up at 2:22 and couldn't go back to sleep so I went to the office to write for a while. He saw my lights on and came down." The explanation seemed so silly as she was relating it.

"Did you know him before that and that's why he came to your place?" Brandon asked.

"No, not really before that night. But my lights were on during the storm; you know, my backup generator." The explanation was getting more and more confusing.

"Yeh, I understand that part, but you let a strange man into your house in the middle of the night?" Brandon's voice was really getting high pitched now.

"Calm down, Brandon. We had sort of met once when he and his dad first moved here, the neighbors had a meet 'n greet BBQ. I went and he was there but we didn't really *meet*. Everybody introduced themselves around the yard and said where we lived, so he knew who I was and I knew who he was, that's all."

"But you let a strange man you barely knew into your house in the middle of the night. I don't believe you sometimes, Julie." Brandon was upset. Julie knew she should have told him before now, but at least it was all out now.

"I know, I know, but it was a terrible thunderstorm and he was soaking wet. I couldn't just let him stand there. He needed help for his dad. He had to call the hospital or something about the machines. And I had my umbrella ready to hit him if necessary, you know the one with the spikey end."

"Yeh, like that would have been any good against a strong man. I don't know what to make of you." Brandon said exasperated with her.

"Brandon, everything turned out alright. We've become friends. And besides, I told him I had a gun."

"A gun?" Brandon's voice was about to become soprano quality again. "Oh boy, what am I going to do with you. It's a good thing I didn't know about this the night of the storm. I would have had a heart attack worrying about you. And what do you mean machines?"

"You don't have to worry about me so much. I can take care of myself." Julie was a little perturbed with him, although she was glad she could always count on Brandon whenever she needed him. "Eric's dad is in a medically induced coma recovering from an accident that I've been telling you about and when the power went off so did the machines, I guess. So, will you call your friend at the police department and see if he can find out any information about that accident?"

"This is quite a story. Why do you need the police to look into it?"

Julie told him about the paper she had accidently seen in Eric's cabinet drawer about a lawsuit and then the news article she saw after she **Googled** the architectural firms in Philadelphia. Something just seemed strange she explained. "It doesn't all add up, does it?"

"You were snooping around in his drawers? I can't believe this!"

"No, I wasn't snooping. I was looking for napkins in the china cupboard while he went down the hall to check on his dad."

"Napkins? What did you need napkins for? Why were you at his house in the first place?" Julie could tell Brandon was really upset. She needed to get him to agree to call his detective friend without saying much more about her and Eric's budding friendship. "We had supper together; I told you a neighbor had invited me. Will you please forget about all that and call your friend?"

Brandon agreed reluctantly. "I suppose so; I don't really know. It does sounds like just an accident. There would have been more in the newspapers or on the news if it wasn't, don't you think?" Brandon was a little perturbed with Julie and this Eric fellow, but still wanted to know more about him and whatever relationship he might have with Julie.

"Well, yes, maybe. It's just that Eric has been so secretive about telling me anything about his career or his dad's accident. He lied to me at first, saying his dad had cancer. Why would he do that unless there is more to the story."

Brandon was worried about Julie getting involved with this Eric guy. "So why are you *seeing* this guy if he's lying to you? I don't like the sound of it, Julie." But he was intrigued now. "You're right. No reason to lie unless you are hiding something. Eric worked for this Folder Architecture and his dad worked for Streeter Construction, and they did the Capitol Avenue Apartments project together, that right?"

"Right, I believe so. So will you call your detective friend?"

"Okay, let me call Don and see if he will check out a few things for us. Stay away from that guy. Call you back later. Love ya."

Julie called, "Love ya, too", as she clicked off.

Julie spent the rest of the day flitting from one project to another without accomplishing much of anything. She started a load of laundry, washed up the breakfast dishes and tried to write a few pages on her new book. By lunchtime she knew she wasn't going to get far on that project. By mid-afternoon, she was starting to bite her fingernails as she waited for Brandon to call back. She had vacuumed the carpet in the living room, bedroom, and her office and **Swiffer** dusted the hardwood floors in the kitchen and hallway. She wanted to call Brandon again and ask if he had talked to his friend, Don, but knew that she shouldn't bother him at work. 'I just have to wait. He'll call when he has any information.' She was just waiting for a pot of Earl Grey to steep when the doorbell rang. Spot ran ahead of her to the door. 'Oh, Brandon,' she thought. 'You didn't need to come down.'

When she opened the door, she was surprised to see Eric Players standing there with her plastic tub with the left over cooking supplies. "You left these," was all he said. He sat the tub down in her foyer and turned and walked away. Julie stood there in surprise watching his back as he marched back up the road. "What's the deal with him?" she said out loud. Spot let out a big meow. "I know, weird?" She picked up Spot and went back to the kitchen to get her cup of tea.

She couldn't understand how things had gone so sour with Eric so quickly. Their friendship had started out great and progressed at a reasonable pace. She knew he liked her and she definitely liked him. The kiss had been something else. Sparks had flown with the electrical charge that ran through her and she knew he had felt it too. 'Why did he pull away so quickly and throw me out? That's a mystery in itself. But one I can't share with Brandon. If we can just find out about the construction accident, then maybe I will have the answers I need.' Julie finished her tea and went to get the plastic tub still sitting on the floor in her foyer. She looked up the street and saw Eric in the yard getting his mail. Just a short time ago, she would have waved and he would have waved back.

Finally, Brandon called after work. He had talked with his friend, like he promised, and Detective Graverton had said he would see what he could find out. In the meantime, Brandon said he had done some searching himself. He had checked into Folder Architecture and Streeter Construction. He told Julie that Eric had been a well-respected designer with the firm. He had worked on many projects in the Philadelphia area, earned some awards and gained quite a name for himself as well as earning a tidy sum of money over the years.

Julie remembered that Eric had told her he was financially comfortable and didn't need to work. "I assumed as much when I saw his new BMW. And the house is really nice."

"BMW? I guess so." Brandon was a little jealous. Even though he drove a newer model Chevrolet Traverse, it wasn't a classic sports car. He had found several news articles about Eric Players and his architectural designs. He had, in fact, received several prestigious awards for his work. His boss, George Folder, CEO of Folder Architecture had praised Eric's designs in public on many occasions. The news had reported that the Capitol

Avenue Apartments project was the biggest project that Eric had been assigned so far in his career and most likely would result in a sizeable promotion for Eric when it was completed.

Then Brandon went on to tell Julie what he had found out about Streeter Construction. Apparently, Fred Streeter and Streeter Construction had been in the news quite a bit as well. There had been reports of faulty materials and safety issues at several job sites. Streeter Construction could be in a lot of trouble financially and legally if that information became public knowledge. And if the accident at Capitol Avenue Apartments had been his fault, it would have been the ruin of Streeter and probably Eric and Folder Architecture. There would be criminal charges filed for Involuntary Manslaughter if people *were* killed. Brandon told Julie that Don was going to look into it further. If there had been deaths involved, there should be more information and if not, someone had swept it all under the rug and Detective Graverton would want to know who, as well as Julie and Brandon.

"I knew there was something a little odd about Eric and his situation at first, but he seemed like such a nice guy, you know, taking care of his disabled father and all. I guess you never know about someone until you get closer." Julie told Brandon.

"Well, don't get any closer to that guy. He sounds like trouble to me. What's the deal with his dad in a medically induced coma anyway? How long do they do that sort of thing? When did he get injured?"

"I don't really know for sure, but I am guessing it was when the building collapsed at the Capitol Avenue Apartments site last year." Julie said.

"So you know that his dad was working there at that time?"

"I'm sure he was. Eric said he and his dad worked together a lot on projects that he designed. His dad was the construction crew manager on the sites."

"Do you suppose Eric's dad had something to do with the faulty materials and safety issues that Streeter was in trouble for?" The picture was getting clearer for Brandon.

"That's what I'm thinking now too. I sure hope Detective Graverton finds out more."

"Me too, I'll call you as soon as I hear. Bye, Julie, love ya."

Julie was disturbed by the information Brandon had relayed. She knew that Eric was keeping a secret of some kind, but she certainly hadn't thought it was illegal or possibly criminal! 'Oh, boy, what if Eric's dad had been responsible and he and Eric were covering it up?' Julie remembered the news article that had said there probably were people killed when the building collapsed. There would definitely be repercussions from that.

Julie wanted to talk to Eric. How could a sweet guy like him be involved in something as underhanded as the collapse of a building where people were injured and killed. She couldn't wrap her head around the idea that the Eric Players she knew would be involved in something like that. Maybe when she got more information from Brandon and his friend she would go talk to Eric. There were always two sides to every story. Surely Eric had moved to Indiana to get away from reporters digging for more information about the accident. Had Eric quit his job or been fired? That was a good question too. Whatever the answer to that question was, she needed to know why he had suddenly dumped her when their relationship had been exploding like fireworks.

When a week went by and Brandon had not called, she decided to call him even if he did get upset with her. He answered right away, "Hey, Julie, how ya doing today?"

"I'm doing okay. I haven't heard from you and I've been wondering if you had any information yet?"

"I'm sorry, it's been busy at work and I just talked to Don briefly. There's a little information, but it's sketchy at this point. Don says the lawyers for Streeter and Folder kept the incident out of court and out of the newspapers as much as possible, so there isn't much to report yet. I guess there was a settlement made to keep both Streeter Construction and Folder Architecture in operation. They agreed to share the costs of rebuilding and the insurance settlements for the injured and the families of the deceased. The only way they could accomplish that is for someone to take the blame for the accident and my guess is, Eric Players as the architect, became the lucky sucker who got that honor. He probably had to agree to sign a document stating he had made a mistake in the design. Unfortunately, Folder would probably have let him go and Eric would lose his license too. Too bad really, if that's the case. I guess that's the bulk of it for now. Don's going to call me when he gets more."

"Oh, my gosh. I feel terrible. I want to go talk to him."

"No, don't do that, Julie. Don't you think it would be best to just stay out of it?" Brandon didn't want her anywhere near Eric until his friend found out more information. The guy might be trouble if Julie confronted him.

Brandon didn't know about Julie and Eric's kiss and she didn't intend to tell him, but she did want to discuss it with Eric. Maybe after she told Eric she knew the truth and that she understood his reluctance to get involved with someone, they could start their relationship over. She could still feel the flame from that burning kiss when she thought about it and her cheeks would suddenly flush bright red. She had to know for sure if Eric still felt the same. She was sure she hadn't imagined the spark between them.

Julie thought about how to approach Eric all week. Should she maybe wait until they ran into each other? It was a small town and there was the bank, the post office, or the grocery store as possibilities. Or she could just go ring his doorbell.

Julie thought about it and decided maybe she should wait a while. It had seemed pretty final that Eric didn't want to see her anymore when he dropped off her plastic tub with the extra cooking supplies. She didn't really need them, just a bit of flour, milk, eggs, some Crisco for baking the roast, oil and seasonings for the Brussels. None of it was important and he could have just kept them. She was surprised to see that he had even put in the flan and the bottle of wine she had brought. The only thing he had said was "You left these," and walked away. She hadn't even had time to respond. She could still hear his voice playing over and over in her mind and how she had just stood there in shock, with Spot meowing loudly. What in the world had happened to make Eric take such a drastic turn? She wouldn't know unless she talked to him. She was just going out the door when the phone rang.

It was Brandon. "Julie, I found out a little more from Detective Graverton. He said Fred Streeter has had several citations and there was a pending lawsuit from another project on file at the courthouse in another nearby town in Pennsylvania. That could be the reason he wanted to keep the Capitol Avenue Apartments incident out of court and the newspapers. You can go on line to the **Philadelphia Inquirer.** It's from the 2/22 edition last year. It's not much of an article, but it's interesting. It talks about problems with inferior rebar and concrete. I don't know much about that sort of stuff but, you check it out. I think there have been lots of problems with Streeter Construction in the past and the Capitol Avenue Apartments was just another. Only this time, two people were killed. Wouldn't you think Folder Architecture's investor would have known about the other lawsuit and been a bit more cautious about giving the bid to them?"

"Hmmm. Well, maybe Eric helped get them approved. If his dad was going to be the crew boss on the construction site, Eric probably thought he could monitor the project and make sure Streeter didn't pull any of their usual shenanigans. He might have given them a glowing recommendation so they would get the bid."

Brandon agreed. "Sure, and if Eric was responsible for getting Streeter the bid in the first place, he probably was in real trouble after the accident."

"Yes, he told me he wasn't working as an architect anymore, but he didn't say why. Do you suppose he was fired?"

"I would certainly think so. If Streeter and Folder had to brunt the costs of the accident, neither company would want him involved in any way. I'm absolutely sure now it was part of the agreement in order to settle out of court. The lawyers did a damn good job of keeping it out of the papers too. As big of an accident as it was, with people injured and killed, whew!"

They talked for a while longer. Brandon said he would see if Don had found out anything else and he would let her know.

He ended with "Stay away from that Eric guy. I don't want him anywhere near you."

"Sure, Brandon." Julie had said, but she didn't make any promises. She still wanted to talk to Eric. Surely there was a plausible explanation for everything. She was beginning to understand why he didn't want to get involved right now, but she hoped after they talked and she told him that she understood, that would change. She would tell him that his secret was safe with her. Of course, she wouldn't tell him about Brandon and Detective Graverton's ongoing search.

Julie returned to working on her new book. Richard had called asking for the final chapters. She fibbed telling him that she had a touch of the flu and hadn't felt like writing. Richard had raved about the first few chapters and she had received his pre-edit comments. He liked the premise and was glad that she was including a bit of mystery into the standard romance novel. It hadn't been her plan at the beginning, but the night of the thunderstorm and her neighbor ringing her doorbell in the middle of the night had stirred up an idea to add a little twist to the romantic plot.

"Julie," Richard said. "I really like where you are going with the storyline. I can hardly wait to get the ending."

"Thank you, Richard." Julie was pleased that he was pleased. They had a good working relationship so far and she hoped he would want to continue publishing her future books. Tetonkian Romantics wasn't a large publishing company but they had managed a couple of authors who had done well on the market. Julie hoped she would someday have a novel on the best seller list. She knew that was a long way in the future, but a girl could dream. Right now, she just had to have a book that at least made enough money to warrant the trust *and* the advance that Tetonkian had given her.

She felt bad about lying to Richard, but she couldn't tell him that she had been wrapped up in researching information about Eric and her suspicions on the Capitol Avenue Apartments accident. There hadn't been much publicity about it and after all, it was in Philadelphia, so the chances of Richard even knowing about it was remote. No sense in even mentioning it, so having the flu was the best choice. Of course, Richard had worried about her too.

"Oh, no, Julie. What can I do? Are you resting and drinking lots of fluids? I can have Natasha make you some chicken noodle soup and Brandon can bring it down. She makes the best soup. It will have you up on your feet in no time. Well, not on your feet, just at the computer!" Richard laughed at his little joke.

"That's not necessary, Richard. I'm much better. I didn't even tell Brandon that I was sick and you don't need to tell him, either. You know how he worries about me. So please don't say anything."

Richard promised. "It will be our little secret. You just take care of yourself and get to finishing that new book. I'm dying to read the end."

"Thank you, Richard. I promise; I'm on it!" Julie told him and bid him farewell. "Got to go before the keys get cold. Bye for now."

Julie put Eric Players and the confusing chain of events out of her mind for the next few days as she worked on the ending of her new book. Richard's phone call had sparked a new surge of writing. 'Funny how a little compliment can encourage you', she thought. She could clearly see the characters and their development. Her fingers were flying over the keys and she barely stopped to eat and sleep for the following four days. Spot had sat in his basket next to her desk and looked at her like she was a crazy person spending so much time there.

As she was wrapping up the final chapter, Julie decided to take a quick break and get a cup of tea. "Hi, my sweet boy," she said as she picked up Spot to snuggle and stroke his fur. "Am I disturbing you?" She carried the cat to the kitchen and put the tea kettle on. "Are you hungry? I am, let's have a snack." She opened the cupboard where she kept the cat food and treats and Spot gave out a little meow. "Oh, so you *do* want a snack? You have been a good boy letting me work without interruption." She put him on the floor and filled his water dish and got out a handful of his favorite kibble bits and proceeded to make a sandwich for herself.

The tea kettle started whistling and Julie hummed to herself as she made a cup of tea and a tuna sandwich. She knew Spot would enjoy licking the can.

By 2:22 PM the next day, Julie had finished the new book. She was pleased with it and felt like it was her best work to date. She hoped Richard would like the surprise ending. When she had looked at the clock on her desk as she hit save on the computer, she was puzzled to see the time. What was with this 2:22 thing? What did her birthday have to do with writing her new book?

Thinking back, she realized it had all started the night of the big thunderstorm when she had met Eric Players. She thought back to the other times the number had appeared. The mileage on

Stormy when she bought her was 22,200 and Eric was with her. Then the date of the news article about the building collapsing in Philadelphia; wasn't that 2/22? And now the clock again just as she was finishing her new book. It didn't make sense, but it was unnerving to think that her birthdate and Eric and the construction accident were all connected somehow.

Julie sent the final chapters of her book to Richard and then called Brandon.

"Hi Julie. What's up?" Brandon was always happy to hear from her in spite of being swamped at work.

"I'm done, done, done with the new book," Julie exclaimed excitedly. "I just sent it off to Richard. I'm sure he will be telling you soon. Oh, what a relief to have it finished."

"I'll bet it is. I know Richard has been pushing you to get it finished. I hope he wasn't too hard on you. He can get pretty tough when there is a deadline for printing." Brandon really liked his boss, but knew him to be a demanding executive at times.

"No, he was fine. He was supportive, but firm. He gave me so many compliments that I got fired up to do it. I'm afraid I got sidetracked a bit in checking about that construction accident in Philadelphia, which, by the way, something is really strange." Julie was uncertain about whether to tell Brandon about her birthdate connection, but maybe there was a simple explanation that just hadn't occurred to her. When she told him, he was as perplexed as she was.

"That is really weird. What possible connection could there be?"

"I don't know, but it all started the night I met him and then it's really spooky about the mileage on my car and then the date of the newspaper story about the accident. I think I should go talk to him."

"Why? I don't think that's a good idea, Julie. When did you last see him?" Brandon wanted to talk her out of going to see Eric.

Julie didn't want to tell him about the kiss and Eric's bizarre reaction but he already knew about the supper so she could mention that. "The night I had supper at his house."

"So, was there anything unusual that night? Did he say anything that was suspicious?"

"Just the court paper I told you I saw in the china cupboard drawer. But, he doesn't know I saw it. I'm going to go over there and talk to him."

"Julie, I wish you wouldn't." Brandon wished he lived closer; he would have come immediately to go with her. "I can't get away from work right now, Julie. Wait 'til I can come down and we can go together. I don't want you going there and bringing up the subject of the accident alone. Who knows how he will react." Brandon was really worried about that possibility.

"Brandon, don't worry about me so much. I just need to talk to him. He probably wouldn't tell me anything with you there. I need to talk to him alone." Julie wanted to clear the air with Eric more about the kiss and his abrupt dismissal of her rather than the construction accident, but she couldn't tell Brandon that. "I'll let you know in a day or two what I find out. There's probably a good explanation, something we haven't even considered. Get back to work and quit treating me like a baby. I'm a big girl now."

"Big girls get into trouble too, you know. Ok, I can't talk you out of something once your mind is made up. So, do what you need to do, then call me afterward, so I know you are okay. Bye, love ya." Brandon hung up but his thoughts were still with Julie throughout the rest of the day. He'd never met this Eric guy, but he knew he didn't like him.

Brandon's intercom rang. It was Richard. "Hey, Brandon, come over to my office when you get a minute."

"Sure, be there in a second." Brandon knew that Richard wanted to talk about Julie's new book. He was anxious to get his copy to read. Brandon hoped it would be the best seller that Julie was hoping for. She deserved it. She had been working hard at her writing career. Journalism hadn't worked out and even though she loved teaching, particularly the kids, he knew her passion was in writing and he was thrilled to see she was on the verge of success.

CHAPTER 11

Julie didn't know what to say to Eric for sure. Should she just call him on the phone? 'No, he'd probably hang up on me. If I'm going to get any answers, I'd best do it in person.' She headed to the kitchen to mash a pot of tea and Spot was under her feet again as he had been all day and she stepped on him. He let out a yowl. Whenever she had gotten up from her desk, he had been right there. She almost tripped over him a couple of times earlier. He was more verbal than usual too. He'd meowed several times at her. She picked him up and said, "What's the matter with you, my sweet boy? You are not acting like yourself. Are you hungry? Didn't I fill your bowl this morning?" She carried the cat to the kitchen and put him down while she started the tea kettle. She reached into the cupboard for Spot's food and filled his water bowl. After she placed his food dish on the floor, he didn't even go near it. "Are you sick, buddy? Do we need to go to the vet?" She decided to clean out the litter box, but didn't see anything unusual there. "Well, if you don't eat by tomorrow, we will make a trip to Doc Waterson to get you checked out.

As Julie waited for the tea kettle to boil, she thought again about Eric. She needed to talk to him. In a moment her mind was made up. She turned off the stove and said to Spot. "You be good and I'll be back in a little while." Spot meowed loudly back at her and Julie shook head. 'What's up with that cat today?' She grabbed her jacket and headed out the front door to walk up to Eric's house.

She had decided she would start with an apology to see if he would even let her in the house. She was prepared for him slamming the door in her face, but still wanted to risk it to see him again. Her thoughts went back to that evening and how much fun they had cooking together and enjoying the meal. He hadn't seemed upset when she had asked to meet his dad. And when they walked up the hallway together with his arm around her, she had felt that he was feeling the same way as she was. Then when he had taken her into his arms and kissed her with so much passion, she knew she wasn't imagining it. He had wanted that kiss as much as she did; she was sure of it! She could feel it in the way he held her and the way his hands had felt on her body. The kiss had been soft and gentle, then grew in intensity until they both were breathless when he broke away. But, the way he escorted her out the door a few seconds later was a complete shock! She had to ask; she just had to ask him why.

Eric saw Julie walking up the street and he wasn't sure what to do. He had hoped she had gotten the message that he wasn't interested when he had dramatically led her to the door. Later when he had taken her things back to her house, he made sure there was no explanation or contact. He just dropped them off and left. Surely, she would realize that he didn't want to pursue a relationship. But, of course, he should never have kissed her; he knew that. He had given away his feelings in that kiss. She was a beautiful sexy woman and he couldn't help himself. Their times together had been fun and easy and he had felt there could be something more. If only he didn't have the accident and his involvement hanging over his head, he could maybe make a life here in Monique with this wonderful woman. 'No use thinking that, stupid.'

Julie saw Eric looking out the window as she approached his house. Would he even answer the door she wondered? But, before she could push the doorbell, Eric opened the door. "What do you want?"

"Umm, could we talk?" Julie asked.

"I don't think there is anything to talk about."

"You don't?" Julie was dumbfounded. "You kiss me passionately and then shove me out the door? Don't you think I deserve at least an explanation? We have been developing a good relationship the past few weeks and then boom, that's it! Can I come in or do I have to stand here and let the neighbors wonder what's going on?" Julie stood there on the doorstep feeling stupid. Why did she want to pursue something that he obviously did not want pursued?

"You're right. I don't need more nosy neighbors asking questions. Come in." Eric stepped back and opened the door wider and Julie walked in past him.

"Oh, so now I'm a nosy neighbor? Eric, what happened? Can we have a cup of tea and talk for a minute?" Julie felt like she was beginning to beg, but at least he had let her in the house. That was a start. She was determined to get answers before she left.

"I suppose." Eric led the way to the kitchen and put the tea kettle on to boil. He sat down at the island counter and Julie sat down next to him. Neither of them talked. He just looked at her and she looked at him. The silence filled the room. Somebody needed to talk first. Finally, Eric said, "I don't know what you want me to say. The kiss was a mistake and I thought it was best to nip it in the bud right then."

"I understand that maybe we were moving too fast, but we were developing a terrific friendship. It was fun and easy and if you thought we should ease off; you could have just told me. I can deal with that, but to literally push me out of the door after you've kissed me that way." Julie was exasperated.

"I know. I am sorry about that. I panicked. Getting into a relationship was not something I planned on when I moved here to Monique. I just wanted a place away from Philadelphia where I could take care of my dad in peace without nosy neighbors asking questions."

"There you go again calling me a nosy neighbor. I'm your friend." Julie wanted him to know that she would still be his friend even if he didn't want a serious relationship.

"I don't need any friends." Eric jumped up when the tea kettle starting whistling. Julie wondered what he was so nervous and adamant about. He didn't seem like the Eric Players she had met a few weeks ago. What was going on? She didn't want to ask since he had commented twice on nosy neighbors asking questions. Maybe with a cup of tea and a little friendly conversation, he would finally open up.

Eric poured them both a cup of tea and got the sugar and cream for Julie's. "You remembered," she said with a chuckle. "Yep." Eric laughed too.

Julie was glad to see he was responding a bit. His joking was a good start. "Thank you." Julie said as he handed her the cup. She felt like he was relaxing and acting more like the Eric she knew. "Hey, I finished my new book." Julie hoped a change in the subject might help.

"That's great. When will it be printed?"

"Not for a while yet. I will get the edits and then I will make some changes and corrections. I will probably have a couple more meetings with my publishing agent as we hash out the things I don't want to change and he does. You know, back and forth until we agree on everything. It's all part of the process. But I think it will go well. Richard Beasley is a great guy. I'm lucky to have him as my agent. My friend Brandon works with him and he helped me get Richard as my agent."

"There's a lot I don't know about getting a book published. Good thing I'm not writing one." They laughed together and for a moment it felt like it had before the kiss and the shove out the door.

"Eric, I'm sorry if I made you feel uncomfortable. I was ready for a kiss, but I understand if you weren't. Our friendship means a lot to me and we could continue being a friends and if something develops later on, I wouldn't object and if it doesn't, I will understand. What do you…."

Julie was interrupted by a loud buzzing sound from down the hall. Eric jumped up and said, "That's one of dad's machines; I've got to check on it." He hurried out of the kitchen and down the hall. Julie sat there for a moment and it occurred to her that this might be a good time to sneak a look at those court papers she had accidently seen in the dining room china cupboard drawer.

She knew she probably shouldn't but her curiosity was getting the best of her. She slipped off the stool and walked quietly to the hallway. She couldn't hear any more buzzing, but she didn't see Eric coming back either. Maybe....

She slid the drawer open as slowly as possible. The papers were still there on top and she lifted them out. *In The District Court of the State of Pennsylvania in and for the City and County of Philadelphia. Docket #222.* Julie let out a little gasp, Docket #222! There was the number again! She suddenly realized why she had been seeing it everywhere and why she had woken up at 2:22 AM on the night of the storm! There was something here she was supposed to find out and her birthdate had given her the clue! Eric was hiding something and she was going to find out what.

She didn't hear him return from the hallway until he said, "Find something you were looking for?" She turned in surprise. "I'm sorry, Eric, I didn't mean to be prying."

"Yes you did. That's why you came here today. You just wouldn't let it go."

"No, it isn't entirely why I came. I want to find out what happened to our friendship."

"Oh, you mean the friendship that allows you to look through my private papers?" Eric's voice was getting tight and tense. Julie could see a strange look in his eyes that made her cringe. She was feeling uncomfortable. She knew that looking through the papers was a mistake. She was never going to regain his trust and friendship now.

"I'm sorry. It's not like that. I accidently saw these papers when I was getting napkins out the night of our supper. I thought we might need some napkins when we had our flan for dessert in the living room. Remember, we were going to have it by the fire with our wine?" Julie knew she was rambling, but she wanted to get back to where they had been a few moments ago, talking like old friends. The look in Eric's eyes though sent a chill down her back and all she wanted to do now was turn and run to the door and get away from him as fast as she could.

Eric could see that Julie was about to bolt for the door and he reached out and grabbed her arm. "Where are you going, sweet lady?"

"I'm sorry, Eric. I shouldn't have been intruding, I know. I was just curious about your dad's accident and when I saw those papers, I thought they might tell me," Julie stammered as she tried to pull away from Eric's grip on her arm. He tightened his hold. "Eric, you're hurting me."

"Well, I knew there would be nosy neighbors here. Just like Philadelphia. People just won't leave it alone; always butting into other people's business. You make one innocent mistake and they never let you forget it." Eric pulled Julie to him and kissed her fiercely. It wasn't the soft passionate kiss like before; it was brutal and harsh and Julie whimpered as he released her lips. "Oh, don't want to kiss me now, huh?"

Julie tried again to reason with him. "Eric, what has gotten into you? You can tell me. I will understand. I apologize for being nosy, but I just want to help." She could see the look in his eyes and he wasn't the same Eric Players she had known earlier. There was something strange about him now and she was beginning to feel afraid.

"Oh, sure, that's what they say at first. They're sorry it happened. 'But we can't keep you on here at Folder anymore,

Eric.' Fifteen years of good work and a chance for a promotion and one little accident and it's all gone. Then your friends say they understand, sure, then why don't they stand by you? They make excuses when you call them to get together, then they quit answering your calls at all."

Julie wanted him to release her arm, it was beginning to hurt more. If she could only get him to let her go. She spoke calmly. "Tell me about it, Eric. I will listen and still be your friend."

Eric's eyes were looking glassy and glazed over like he was in a trance and he mumbled something about his dad. Julie thought that was her opportunity to ask. "What about your dad, Eric? Was he responsible for the accident?"

Eric shook himself and looked at her. "No, Streeter was. It was his company that was using crappy materials trying to save money on the project and get the building done on schedule. I tried to tell dad that the timeframe wouldn't work. I showed him the change orders for the rebar and I knew it wouldn't be strong enough. He swore to me that he would talk to Streeter. They had been friends for years and dad had done many projects with him. I know that dad knew that Streeter used inferior products sometimes and cut corners. I told him nothing good would come of it, but he just got mad at me. I wanted to tell George Folder, but if I did my dad would be in trouble and all I wanted was for the Capitol Avenue Apartments to be finished so dad could get out of there. I never wanted the building to collapse. I never dreamed it could."

As he related the incident, Eric relaxed his hold on Julie's arm and she eased away and he released her. She knew she should make a run for the door, but Eric was standing there as great sobs started shaking his body. She wanted to help. She put her arms around him and said, "It will be alright Eric, as soon as your dad is better, we can talk with Streeter and Folder and straighten this all out."

"No," Eric shouted and jerked away from her. "Don't you understand; it can't be straightened out. People died and my dad and I are responsible. We both knew what might happen and did nothing to stop it. That's murder; we'll go to jail. I didn't want it to be true. I tried to reason with dad, but he wouldn't tell me the truth at the time. Then the building came down and he was injured. All I could do then was try to find out what happened while he recovered. And when I did, there was really nothing more I could do. I couldn't change things. I had signed the settlement papers and everyone went on as if nothing had happened. But it didn't really for us and it was all my fault." Eric let out a huge sigh as he finished.

Julie was glad he was finally opening up. She knew that he would be better now that it was all out there. "Eric, let's go sit down and we can talk some more." She wanted him to understand that she would remain his friend no matter what the future might bring.

"I don't want to talk about it anymore. There's nothing to talk about and there's nothing anyone can do. It's over. You should have stayed out of it. Now I have to do something about you." Eric's face took on a strange sinister look.

'What did he mean, do something about me?' Julie felt a sudden chill run through her like it had the night she had first met Eric when he was a stranger at her door during the storm. Now he felt like a total stranger; someone she had never met before and certainly someone she never wanted to kiss ever again as long as he was going to continue talking like that! She didn't know for sure what his intentions were, but it didn't sound good. She backed slowly towards the front door, but Eric caught her arm again. "Where you going, my sweet lady? Trying to leave again. I can't let you do that."

There was that tone again that he had used earlier. It was frightening. She felt certain now that Eric wasn't going to listen or do any more talking. He grabbed her arm tighter and pulled her down the hallway. She struggled to get free to no avail. His grip was strong and he dragged her into the spare bedroom at the end of the hall at the back of the house. Julie knew that probably no one would hear her scream as she struggled to free herself from his grasp. Eric must have realized she was contemplating screaming because he reached into the bedside stand and grabbed a large red bandana hanky and plugged her mouth. "That's just in case you get the notion to scream, not that anyone would hear you back here. Quit struggling, I don't want to hurt you, but I will if I have to."

He tied another bandana around Julie's hands behind her back. He threw her on the bed and tied another around her ankles. "So sorry to have to do this to you, my pretty lady." He stroked her face and Julie feared he was going to rape her but all he said was, "That will do until I get something stronger. I have some duct tape in the garage that should do it. You just rest here quietly and I'll be back in a jiffy."

Eric headed up the hallway and out through the kitchen door to the garage. Julie could hear him slamming cabinet doors or tool box lids as he looked for the tape. She knew she was in big trouble. 'Oh, God, how did this happen?' She rolled over on her side as best she could with her arms behind her back and tried to look out the window for help from someone. There was nothing but wooded area beyond the windows and Julie knew the nearest neighbor was up the road further. She struggled to get her hands free and felt the bandana loosening a little.

"Oh, I see you are thinking about leaving me again, huh?" Eric said as he entered the room. "Look what I found in the garage just for you. It's blue too, to match the color of your eyes. Why couldn't you have just left it alone, Julie? I was just getting attached to you. Well, you see that was the problem, wasn't it? I was getting attached. I should never have run to your house in the storm. But what else could I do? Your lights were on and I needed to help dad. Of course, if I hadn't panicked and waited a few minutes, the battery would have kicked in and he would have been fine. Stupid me." Eric proceeded to fasten Julie's hands and feet with the duct tape. He pulled it tight and Julie knew she wouldn't be able to loosen it like she did the bandana. "There we go; snug as a bug in a rug. I always wondered what that meant, now I know. Take a nap, little lady; you're not going anywhere soon." Eric turned, walked out and closed the door behind him.

Julie lay there with tears in her eyes. It was hard to cry with the bandana choking her and she chided herself. 'Stop it, stop it right now. Quit crying and think of what to do. You've got to get to a phone and call for help or get the Hell out of here!' She struggled with the duct tape around her wrists. It wouldn't budge. Eric had made sure of that. Her shoulders were beginning to ache from her arms being behind her back and she tried to adjust a bit to ease the cramp. She attempted to roll over again and scoot to the edge. She scooted too far and fell off the bed! She hit the floor with a thud and lay there shaking and tears began again to roll down her cheeks. 'What was I thinking?'

Eric had heard the thud and came to investigate. "Oh, dear, you are going to be a problem child, aren't you? Ok, then, I need to get some rope, I think. Be right back. Don't go anywhere." His voice had a sing-song lilt and Julie shuddered at the sound. 'What had happened to him?'

He was back in a few minutes with a strong white rope, the kind Julie's mother used to use for a clothesline in the back yard when she was a kid. Julie remembered her mom had said that white rope would stand up to a tornado. Julie wasn't sure about that but she knew it would certainly stand up to holding her to the bed. Eric proceeded to secure her to the headboard. He changed the duct tape to fasten her hands in front so she could lay flat. 'At least he's being a little considerate', she thought. He removed the bandana from her mouth to put duct tape over it instead. Julie tried to bite him and he slapped her. "Now why would you want to bite me?" And Julie realized that he wasn't going to be that considerate!

After he left, Julie was thinking about what to do. Maybe nothing at the moment. There were people who would check on her and if she didn't return their calls, they would surely investigate. Brandon would be calling her soon or surely Richard would. 'That's it. Just lie here quietly and wait it out.' She told herself. 'Brandon will have information to share soon and he'll wonder why I don't answer the phone. If he doesn't reach me then he'll drive down here and find me gone. So, I just need to stay calm and wait.'

It seemed like hours that she laid there and as the sky began to go dark, Julie dropped off to sleep and when she woke it was morning and Eric was there with a tray of food. It smelled good and Julie realized she hadn't had anything to eat since breakfast the day before.

"I've got something for you to eat and if you promise not to bite me when I take off the duct tape, I will feed you." Julie nodded her head. She was hungry and there was no need to die of starvation she decided. Who knew how long he intended to keep her there? "Good, here goes." Eric pulled the duct tape off carefully and Julie stretched her mouth. It was sore where the duct tape had stuck down tightly. "I'm sorry about that, kiddo. But if you would promise not to scream, I could leave it off."

"I'm not going to scream. Besides, didn't you say no one would hear me."

"Smart girl. Ok, what do you want first, egg or toast?"

"I would really like something to drink. My mouth is really dry."

"I fixed your Earl Grey with sugar and cream just like you like it. And we've got scrambled eggs with ham and a slice of toast."

"Wow, this is good room service. I would enjoy it better if I wasn't tied to this bed." Julie said sarcastically.

"Now, now, no need to get testy with me. I'll take good care of you if you promise to be good."

"How long do you intend to keep me here?"

"I don't know yet. I've got to think about it and figure out what I'm going to do. Oh, Julie, why did you have to get involved? I only wanted to move to a small town where no one knew me or anything about the accident so I could be alone with my dad while he recovered and I could get details from him about the accident. I just didn't think he would recover so quickly. He was practically healed by the time I took him out of the hospital. But I was able to convince the doctor that keeping him sedated and comfortable was best while we moved and got settled. The doctor was agreeable and you'd be surprised how easy it is to get all the medical equipment you need. A few searches on the internet and I learned how to do everything to keep him in the medically induced coma for as long as I wanted."

As Eric talked, Julie realized that he had gone completely off the deep end and it scared her to death. He had deliberately put his dad in a coma! What would he do to her? 'Oh, God, please let me get out of this alive!'

'Think fast, Julie, think fast.' Her mind was in a whirl. "Eric, I need to go to the bathroom. I haven't been all night. I can't eat breakfast if I don't go."

"What? Oh, no. I can't let you up; you'll try to run away." Eric shook his head in confusion. 'Wouldn't she try to make a run for it if he untied her. Could he trust her?'

"No, I won't try anything, but I do need to go. Please?" Julie pleaded and hoped he would understand her need to go to the bathroom. "You can stand outside the door and then tie me up again afterwards." She remembered there was a window in the bathroom and she could possibly get out of it. She fully intended to get away.

"I can't do that, Julie. You know about the window in there and you will try to leave me again, won't you?" Eric's voice almost sounded like a frightened little boy. His eyes had taken on that glazed look again.

"No, I won't Eric, I promise. I just need to go to the bathroom really bad." She felt she wasn't making much headway with him. Then suddenly he smiled and got up from the bed.

"I'll get a **Chux** to put under you. That will work. I have some in dad's room. Be right back." Eric sat the breakfast tray on the night stand and turned and walked out the door up the hallway.

Julie's mind was whirling. 'Oh, my God, he's going to let me wet through my clothes.' Eric was back in a minute with a large box of **Chux** pads. He lifted Julie's bottom and tucked two of them under her as expertly as a nurse. Then, as if it was his usual routine, he pulled down her slacks and underpants. 'Oh, Lord help me. Don't let him rape me.' Julie wanted to scream but feared he might do something worse if she did, so she just turned her head away from him as tears rolled down her cheeks. This was the most humiliating thing that had ever happened to her! Eric gently placed a blanket over her lap like it was the most natural thing in the world and said, "Don't cry now, I've made it all better; you can go whenever you please and then we can have our breakfast."

Julie didn't think she could eat OR urinate at the moment. She was supposed to just go in the Chux? Eric had completely lost all sense of reality! How in the world could he do that? He wasn't the same person she had known a few weeks ago. It was like he was in some sort of weird trance. She was terrified; then, without her being aware of it, her bladder relaxed and she did release.

As she laid there on the Chux with her clothes pulled down around her ankles, Eric continued to smile while he fed her the scrambled eggs bite by bite as if she was a child. She really didn't want to eat but refusing him might send him into a rage. God only knew what he would do if she made him angry again. She had seen how quickly his mood could change. When she thought about how she had actually wanted him to take her bed, she cringed. This certainly was not what she had in mind!

Eric chatted casually as he fed her and shared a couple of bites himself. It was just like they were having a normal meal together talking about the weather and the news. Eric told her he had seen a robin building a nest in the small tree outside his kitchen window and he said he had watched the robin as she built, then laid her eggs. There were four little blue eggs he told her and he talked easily about waiting for them to hatch.

Julie couldn't believe it; he was insane! She managed to choke down a few bites and when it was finished, he said, "I have a few errands to run so I will be gone for a little while. Will you be a good girl while I am gone?" Julie could only nod in response, the tears she was fighting back were welling up in her throat. She didn't want him to see her crying; it might send him into another level of craziness. Julie realized he must be schizophrenic and if anything upset him, it could be disastrous.

Julie heard the garage door opening and the sound of the car pulling away. She struggled against the rope and the duct tape on her wrists to no avail. He had definitely made sure she wasn't going anywhere. She laid there listening to the hum of the machines across the hall and a clock ticking somewhere close by. There were birds chirping outside her window and she suddenly thought of Spot alone at the cottage! He would wonder where she was. She never left him alone at night. She thought back on yesterday afternoon and remembered how Spot had clung so close by her all day and how he had meowed when she was leaving. It was like he knew something was wrong. She always heard that animals had a sense about things. 'Too bad I'm not as smart as my cat' she thought as she struggled at the duct tape again. If she could only get her hands free! She did manage to pull her arms up to her mouth and began to chew on the edge of the tape. 'Thank you Lord, for letting him not re-tape my mouth. At least I convinced him I wouldn't scream.'

She struggled to tear off a large strip and would have gotten it completely off if she hadn't heard the garage door opening again. There wasn't enough time! She quickly tried to tuck her hands under the blanket he had laid over her earlier for privacy. She heard his footsteps coming down the hall. Eric opened the door, "I'm back; miss me?" Julie couldn't bring herself to respond. His cheerful sing song voice made her sick. She just closed her eyes.

"Oh, now, pretty lady, are you mad at me for leaving you alone? I promised I wouldn't be gone long, didn't I?" He came over to her at the side of the bed. "I probably need to change those **Chux,** huh?" Julie turned away. She couldn't bear the insult again and she didn't want Eric to see the humiliation and pain on her face. 'Just stay calm,' she told herself. She didn't care how good of a nurse he had become taking care of his dad, she didn't need or want him changing her! She tried to lay still hoping he wouldn't notice the chewed ends of the duct tape around her wrists. Her heart was beating wildly with fear and disgust.

When he lifted the blanket, he knew immediately what she had been trying to do. "Oh, Julie, you weren't trying to escape again? You are being a bad girl." His voice sounded like he was disciplining a small child. "You know, I didn't want to have to do this, but you've made it impossible for me to just keep you tied up. I didn't want to use the duct tape, but I have to in case you wake up when I'm gone."

Julie didn't know what he was talking about. "I said I wouldn't yell and I haven't, you know that." She was frightened about what he might be thinking and planning. "Really, Eric, I promise I will be good and not try anything again, please." Julie sobbed as he put the duct tape over her mouth again.

"Yes, but you can't really be trusted, can you, my sweet little lady. So pretty, but not very faithful. It's a good thing I went to the drug store to refill dad's prescription. Now I know you will not be getting away."

Julie saw the needle coming towards her and struggled to pull away. She felt the prick in her neck and everything went silent and dark.

CHAPTER 12

Don Graverton was a Detective with the Fort Wayne Police Department and a good one. He had been with the force for 16 years, right out of college and had moved from the ranks of Rookie to Detective in no time. The guys at the precinct had given him the nickname of "Don Done" because if a case was assigned to Don, he got the job done! Don thought it was silly, but it had stuck. Everyone knew him by that name and he finally came to accept it. He knew it was meant in fun but with respect.

He didn't look like you would expect a police detective to look; short stocky build, brown crew cut hair, black rimmed glasses that made him appear somewhat studious, but not particularly intelligent, not the kind of guy who would stand out in a crowd. And that's what made him a good detective because he wasn't the stereotype in everyone's mind. No fugitive would ever think that he could outrun them or outsmart them. But Detective Graverton had been third in his graduating class in college, not because he couldn't have been first, but because he hadn't wanted the limelight. When he started at the Fort Wayne Police Department, he made detective long before the other want-a-bees there, because he kept his cool in any situation and played it low.

He never failed to solve his cases because he was diligent like the old tortoise and the hare story. The other guys were jealous at times, but they chipped in and got him a khaki trench coat when he made detective and joked that he was **Columbo**. Even though they kidded him, they also knew that Don Graverton was a man they could count on.

When Brandon had called to ask if he could look into something for him, Don didn't hesitate. He and Eric had been friends a long time. They had gone to college together at **Purdue** in Fort Wayne where Brandon had studied Journalism and Publishing and Don majored in Criminal Justice. They were miles apart in almost all their interests except for when it came to basketball. They had met at a **Boilermakers** game and became fast friends. They were over-the-top fans of **Robbie Hummel**, **Purdue's** star forward. There had been many a bet over how many points Robbie would score in a game with the loser buying the beers. Brandon had bought his fair share over the years. Don was as good at predicting basketball game scores as he was a detective.

Don liked to brag that he knew Robbie personally because they had both gone to High School in **Valparaiso,** when in actuality Don's only contact with Robbie was the time he bumped into him in the hallway after a game, but Don diligently stuck to his story! They hadn't even been in high school at the same time, but an alumni was an alumni and Don swore by that connection.

Brandon and Don had both worried about Robbie's previous lower back injury and were thrilled when Robbie was selected for the USA Men's World University Games in Belgrade, Serbia in 2009. Oh, how they had wanted to go, but their careers were just taking off and they couldn't get away or afford it at the time so they had to be content with watching the news reports.

They had been intrigued about Robbie and Jeffrey Jordan, MJ's oldest son, who Robbie got to know through playing in the Nike All-American games. Their favorite story was about how Robbie got to meet his idol in Las Vegas because of his friendship with Jeffrey.

The story on Google goes: *Hummel was just home from Spain where he had been playing when a friend set him up at the Aria Hotel in Vegas and had asked Robbie if he would like to play in a golf game with Michael Jordan. It was a chance of a lifetime! The golf game later got nixed and Robbie thought his opportunity to meet Air Jordan, his favorite player, was over. Later, though, Robbie and his friends walked into the bar at the Aria and there was MJ himself! Robbie wanted to meet him so he decided to muster the courage to approach Michael and ask about Jeffrey. Robbie told himself to just act normal and say 'Hello' and ask about his friend. He was nervous; after all, he was going to talk to <u>thee</u> Michael Jordan. But before Robbie could even say his name, Michael saw him approaching and said, "Robbie Hummel, my man, what's up, dude?" Robbie said it was crazy; he was so happy. Michael Jordan knew him! The two only talked for about 5 minutes but Robbie had said meeting Michael Jordan was a moment he would never forget.*

Brandon and Don loved that story and tried to outdo each other in the telling of it. And no matter whose version got told, their friendship had lasted through the years after college because of their love of Robbie Hummel and that story. They would call each other if they heard any news about Hummel and get together to talk about it over a couple of burgers and beers. Don had gotten married a few years ago and his wife had a baby, so they hadn't seen each other for a while, but, when Brandon had called to ask Don to look into the construction accident in Philadelphia, although he wondered why, he said yes immediately. If Brandon needed something, Don was ready to help in any way he could. Their friendship was still strong no matter how long it had been. Besides, Don thought 'I can show him pictures of my boy, the one who's going to be a basketball star when he grows up. Gonna, be just like Robbie Hummel.'

They agreed to meet for dinner downtown at **BJ's Restaurant & Brewhouse**. It had been their favorite hangout during college and for several years after college they had met there for a hamburger and a couple of beers. Even though the original owners had passed away and new owners were running the place, the guys still loved the atmosphere. The food wasn't quite as good as it had been back in their college days. They never ordered the cheese curds anymore; they just weren't the same, but they could still reserve their favorite booth where they could talk and laugh in private.

When Brandon explained the situation to Don about Julie and how she was concerned about a guy who had moved to Monique and lived up the road from her, Don was ready to get on it. He did vaguely remember hearing about a construction accident in Philadelphia where a building had collapsed at the site and several workers were injured and some killed. There hadn't been much in the newspapers about it, just the initial item on the local news when it first happened. Don was more than happy to help his friend. He would see if he could find out the details through his connections in the police department.

"So what do you think about this guy?" Don had asked. "Was he involved in something illegal that caused the accident?"

"I don't know; that's what I want you to find out." Brandon's face showed his concern. "I'm worried about Julie. You know how she is; she's a writer and her curiosity always gets her involved if there is a mystery."

Don could tell his friend was worried about Julie. He tried to lighten the moment. "Yeh, I remember she was a pain in school. She drove you nuts when you worked on the campus paper together. I always thought she was going into Journalism though. Didn't she take a job at the **Journal Gazette** right after college? She wanted to be involved in the big breaking news stories."

"Yes, but she got stuck writing the obits, never got to go out in the field on a hot story like she wanted. It was a dead-end position. After two years she left and got her teaching certificate and taught school 'til she resigned to start her writing career."

"Whoa, three careers. She always was an ambitious one." Don took a swig of his second beer and leaned back in the booth. "So how come you two never got together? You were crazy about her in college and you've stayed friends all these years. I would have thought you'd be married with a couple of kids by now."

"I would have liked to but Julie just wanted to be friends. We broke up in High School after going to the prom together. We thought we were going to different colleges at the time, but I changed to **Purdue** after two years to be close to her. Nothing ever happened though. I guess it was too late for anything more than friendship even though she wasn't with anyone else. We never talked about it and we had agreed we should remain friends, so that's how I've handled it. If she ever gave an indication that she wanted something more, I would be right there ready and willing, but she never has. She's never found anyone else, so who knows, maybe someday?"

"That's a bummer, man. I'll pray for you; married life is great especially when you have kids. Here, look at my son, the next Robbie Hummel, I tell ya!"

The two friends laughed and talked about old times a bit longer while they ate, then Don said, "So, tell me, what's the deal with this guy and the construction accident?"

"His name is Eric Players and he worked for Folder Architecture and he was the designer on the building that collapsed, the Capitol Avenue Apartments. His dad, Ben Players, was the crew boss on the project. He worked for Streeter Construction and I did find out a few things about Streeter and some bad dealings in faulty materials. I'm hoping you can find out more details."

"Well, I can certainly see what's out there. Sounds interesting. I got some buddies in the FBI who owe me a favor." Don said.

"Aw, that would be awesome, Don. Thank you so much." I just worry about Julie being friends with this guy and I want to know that she's safe."

"You don't suppose she's romantically involved with him do you?" Don hated to ask, but he wanted to see Brandon's reaction.

"She better not be!" Brandon blurted out then caught himself. "No, I didn't really mean that the way it sounded. Of course, I hope she's not, but if she is, well, she's my friend and I wish her well." Brandon tried to make his response sound convincing. But his friend knew better.

The guys finished their beers and Don said he would call Brandon as soon as he had anything to report. Brandon knew that he could count on Don and when Don called just a week later, Brandon was excited to hear what he had found out.

"Let's meet at BJ's again. I want to go over this info in person," Don said.

"Is it bad?" Brandon asked, fearing the worst.

"Well, yes and no. Let me show you. Can you come tonight about 6:00? I'll reserve our booth."

"Ok, see you then." Brandon hung up the phone with a sickening feeling starting in his gut. 'Why couldn't Don tell him over the phone?' The afternoon seemed to drag by, Brandon couldn't sit still at his desk. He was pacing his office at 2:22 when Richard walked in. "Brandon, what are you doing? The meeting about Julie's new book started at 2:00. Everyone is waiting for you. I've served them coffee and croissants but they are getting antsy waiting for details on your marketing promotion. I told them you were just finishing the presentation. It's done, isn't it? We need these investors in order to get her new book off the ground. Come on." Richard turned and walked out of the office; Brandon grabbed his laptop and headed down the hall to the conference room.

"I'm sorry everyone, something came up and I, I, I...I'm sorry." Brandon stammered. "Just let me get my laptop connected to the screen and you will see what I have in mind to promote Julie Avery's new book." The meeting had gotten off to a rough start, but Brandon got it back on tract and the investors were pleased with his ideas for promoting Julie's book when it came off the presses

Most of them had been pleased when they had read her short stories and were excited to read the new book. Brandon assured them that it was going to be a best seller and would make everyone a lot of money. They really liked Brandon's design for the cover and the picture of Julie for the back cover was remarkable. Her grey/blue eyes sparkled animating her face. Everyone could almost feel the emotion radiating from this lovely young woman and they were excited to be a part of the project.

Brandon shared excerpts from the book and they were surprised that Julie had turned the book into a romance/mystery novel. That was unexpected. Her first book had been a non-fiction WWII novel, but the new book was pure fiction with the heroine in trouble and her long time love saving the day. Brandon refused to tell them the exact ending and the investors were so intrigued that they signed the contract before they left the office. Their lawyers had agreed that it was indeed a good investment, so everyone was happy. Brandon breathed a sigh of relief and Richard patted him on the back. "Good job, Brandon, well done."

Finally, the afternoon was over and Brandon grabbed his backpack when his office clock read ten minutes to 5:00 and he was walking out of the elevator right at 5:00 o'clock pushing his bike to the curb. He fastened his backpack securely and put on his helmet. He had an hour before he was to meet Don at BJ's, but the restaurant was across town and he had to ride his bike in rush hour traffic through the busiest part of Fort Wayne. He wanted to get there and be ready when Don arrived with the information. Brandon was anxious to find out what Don had learned.

He was riding furiously with his head down and was so intent on getting to BJ's that he didn't see the light up ahead change to red. He had been riding fast to keep up with the traffic and when the car stopped in front of him, he didn't. In the blink of an eye he was plummeted over the handle bars of his bike and slammed into the back of the car. He and his bike hit the trunk of the car and then fell to the pavement. The car behind him screeched to a stop, just missing hitting Brandon.

The guy in the car in front heard the thud and looked into his rearview mirror just as Brandon was rolling off the end of the car and into the street. He jumped out and ran to see what had happened. The guy in the car behind got out also and approached Brandon who lay in the street with his bike across his legs, the front tire bent and Brandon sprawled on the pavement nearly unconscious.

"Dude, what happened? Are you alright?" the men leaned over Brandon. "Someone call 911," one of them shouted to the crowd that was gathering when Brandon didn't respond. "This guy isn't moving." Brandon's left ankle was twisted at an odd angle and his forehead had a gash and blood was running down his face. The impact had knocked the air out of him and he couldn't respond although he hadn't totally blacked out. The blood was running into his eyes and he couldn't see the people around him. In the confusion he didn't even know what had happened. There was yelling and people talking to him as a large crowd gathered in the street. Brandon could hear sirens in the distance not realizing they were coming for him.

The ambulance was on the scene in a few minutes and the crowd moved away to let the attendants through. The police were there shortly after the ambulance and began questioning the onlookers and the driver of the vehicle. Brandon's head began to clear as they were loading him into the ambulance and he managed to say, "Tell Don Done...." before he finally gave it up and passed out. The pain and confusion was too much and his head fell back on the gurney as he let the first responders do their job.

When Brandon woke up in **St. Joseph Hospital** Don was there and so was Richard Beasley. Don had called Richard immediately when his buddies at the precinct had called and told him a guy who was injured in a bike accident was calling for Don Done. Don knew immediately it was Brandon. Richard had met Don at the hospital and they were both there when the doctor told them Brandon was awake and they could go in to see him. "Oh, hey, guys." Brandon managed to squeak out weakly. "What happened?"

"You tell us." Richard said. Don called me saying you had been in an accident and you told the police to call him. "Why didn't you call me?" Richard's voice sounded a little hurt that he hadn't been the first one Brandon would call.

"I was on my way to meet Don so I guess he was on my mind, sorry Richard. I do appreciate you being here. Thanks, Don for calling him."

"No problem, buddy. You just rest. We'll stay close." Brandon felt blessed to have such good friends. "Hey, where's Julie? Didn't anyone call her?"

"I tried but no answer." Don said. "So did I, same thing." Said Richard.

"Well, keep trying, I want to see her." Brandon sounded a bit desperate. They both knew that Brandon considered Julie's well-being over his own.

"Calm down, Brandon, the doctor said you would be okay. You're not dying. No need to alarm Julie." Richard said.

"You were pretty lucky there, guy. Downtown traffic at rush hour on a bike and all you get is a bump on the head and a broken ankle. I'd say someone was watching over you." Don told his friend.

"That's good to know, but I need to see Julie. Will you guys keep trying? Where's my phone; I'll call her myself?" Brandon tried to sit up and reach for the night stand, but the pain in his ankle and the throbbing in his head made him flop back down. "Oh, geez, that hurts."

"I imagine it does. So why don't you just go back to sleep. No need to fight those pain pills. The doctor said sleep is what you need the most right now. We'll reach Julie and I'm sure she will be here just as soon as she can."

"But what about our meeting and the information you found?" Brandon suddenly remembered the reason he was frantically riding across town.

"We can go over that later. It's quite a lot and I want to be sure you are clear headed when we do. It can wait 'til you are better." Don told his friend.

"What information?" Richard asked.

"Oh, I've been looking into an old construction accident for Brandon. It's something Julie is involved in." Don answered.

"Julie was in a construction accident?" Richard exclaimed.

"No, no, Julie wasn't in an accident but a new friend of hers was and Brandon asked me to find out more about it." Don didn't really want to go into details with Richard right then, so he hoped

Richard would let it drop. Fortunately, Richard's phone rang and he left the room to answer it.

"Don't tell him anymore, please." Brandon managed to mumble before he faded into a deep sleep from the oxycodone. Don had no intentions of telling Richard anything else and was glad that the phone call had taken Richard out of the room. Richard was still on the phone when Don left Brandon's room and Don gave a quick wave to him as he headed for the elevator. 'Whew, dodged that bullet.' Don took out his phone and tried Julie's number again. Still no answer. 'Where can she be without her phone? Brandon said that's not like her.'

Brandon was sitting up in bed when Don returned the next morning. The breakfast tray was still there but Brandon hadn't touched anything. "I think the doctor will be unhappy to see that you are not eating your breakfast, young man."

"I don't care. I want to get out of here." Brandon answered grumpily.

"Uhhh, buddy, I don't think so. Not today at least. The doctor stitched up your head, but he says you've got a slight concussion and he wants to keep you another day. And he's going to put a cast on your ankle too." Don hated to be the bearer of bad news, but that wasn't the only bad news he had for Brandon.

"Crap, crap, crap!" Brandon banged his hand on the table almost spilling the breakfast tray on the floor.

"Hey, hey. What you doing?" Don jumped up to catch the tray before it slid off the table.

"I can't be here, Don. I need to find out where Julie is." Brandon slumped back onto his pillow.

"I'm sure she's okay. She probably has lost her phone or let the battery go dead or something. Listen, if it will make you feel any better, I'll drive down to Monique and check in on her, okay? "Oh, thank you, Don. That would be great. Let me know as soon as you talk to her." Brandon felt a little better knowing that his friend was going to locate Julie, but he wouldn't rest entirely until he talked to her himself.

"If you feel up to it after you get your cast on, I'll come back this afternoon and we can go over the information I have for you on Eric and Ben Players and Streeter Construction, okay?"

"Yeh, but I want to know about Julie first."

"Sure, buddy, you rest now and I'll head to Monique and I'll be back later today." Don gave his friend a quick pat on his shoulder and left. Brandon reached for his phone and tried Julie's number again. No answer. He was holding the phone when it rang. "Julie?" Brandon said into the phone without looking.

"Nope, Brandon, it's me, Richard. How you doing? No contact from Julie yet, I take it. I've tried her a couple of times this morning with no luck."

"Thanks, Richard. Don is going to drive down to Monique to check on her. I'll let you know when I hear something, okay?"

"Sure, no problem. I hope Don finds out what's going on. Hey, what does the doctor say about your ankle?" Richard asked hoping Brandon wouldn't be laid up too long.

"Got to have a cast, I guess. This afternoon, I think. Then I suppose I'll get to go home on crutches. I'll ask him when I can come back to the office, until then, I probably can do some things from home when my head clears up." Brandon assured Richard.

Richard breathed a sigh of relief. Brandon was his best editor and he didn't want to be without him for long, especially since Julie's book was about to be released. Brandon knew just how to handle the investors and he had personally designed the marketing strategy. "Okay, Brandon, rest and take care. I'll talk to you later."

Brandon laid his phone down just as the nurse entered. "Good morning, Mr. Jenkins. I see you didn't eat any of your breakfast. Won't get your strength back that way. I need to take your vitals and then we'll be off to get that cast on your foot." Brandon didn't answer, he just gave her a scowl. She proceeded to take his temperature and blood pressure. She put the little clamp thing on his finger. "Never did know what that was for," Brandon grumbled more to himself instead of her.

"It's your oxygen level and you seem to be okay so just relax while I record your chart. I think you are good to go for now. I'll take this tray away and go get a wheelchair to take you downstairs. Are you sure you don't at least want the orange juice?" Brandon waved her off and turned away. She took the tray and left. When he turned back he saw that she had left the carton of orange juice there. He reached for it and opened it. It was cold and sweet and tasted good, but he wouldn't admit it to her, he decided stubbornly.

Getting the cast on was less of a project than Brandon had imagined. And it came in several colors. Brandon didn't care what color they gave him so the nurse chose the blue one and he was back in his room in no time. Brandon looked at it and thought the blue reminded him of the color of Julie's eyes, so he was pleased at the nurse's selection.

'Julie! Where was she?' Getting the cast on had temporarily let his worried mind rest about Julie, but when he thought about the cast being the color of her eyes, his fear returned. Don hadn't returned from Monique yet, so Brandon called him. "Don, what's the news about Julie?"

"Nothing to report yet. Hang in there. I will get to the bottom of this. Call you back soon. Just rest for now." Don hoped the nurse would give Brandon another pain pill to knock him out.

Don had gone to Julie's cottage at the end of the cul-de-sac and rang the doorbell. There had been no answer so he walked around the house and peered into several windows. There didn't seem to be anyone there, but he did hear a cat meowing. 'Strange. Why would she go off for a couple of days and leave her cat there alone? Well, I suppose cats can take care of themselves if you leave them food and water and a fresh litter box.'

He tried the garage door but couldn't get in. He wondered if her car was there and she had left with someone else, but no luck getting in and there were no windows in the garage. He checked all the doors and windows on the cottage and everything was locked. 'Good girl, Julie. Living at the end of this cul-de-sac with the woods beyond, it's a good idea to keep doors and windows locked.' Don didn't really know Julie that well since it had been a long time since they were in college, so he had no clues as to where she might be. 'Monique is her hometown so maybe there's family nearby she's visiting. But that doesn't explain why she's not answering her phone. I can't imagine she wouldn't take it with her.' Don called Julie's number again and listened at the door to see if the phone rang inside. When he heard the Star

Trek theme playing, he chuckled. 'Leave it to her to do that.' But the humor quickly turned to concern. 'Now I know something *is* wrong; no one goes far for very long without their phone.'

He left his car parked at Julie's cottage and walked up the road to the next house. The woman who answered the door was a Mrs. Chatterly who proved to live up to her name. She said she knew Julie but that she hadn't seen her in a few days. They didn't socialize much and the only time she saw her was if she drove by in her little red car or if they happened to see each other at the grocery store.

"She's a writer, you know and she works from home so she's not out daily like she was when she was teaching school. She pretty much keeps to herself. I've tried to get to know her better, when she first bought her house, but she's a loner, never wanted to come over for coffee. I called her several times, but she was always busy, or so she said. Guess, she's not so busy now, 'cause I do know she's been seeing our new neighbor." The woman pointed at the house across the street. "I've seen her coming and going a few times. He's quite good looking and they would make a nice couple, I think. I don't know why a pretty young woman such as her isn't married with a couple of kids. Well, maybe they'll get married and have some. Sorry, I can't help you much. Would you like to come in for a cup of coffee?"

"Thank you, ma'am, but I really don't have time. I do appreciate yours." Don gave a little bow and stepped back on the front porch.

"Oh, well, everyone's always too busy to share a little of their time. Why don't you go ask Mr. Players?" Mrs. Chatterly said as she was closing the door.

"Who?" Don asked. He had been half listening to the woman as she rambled on about marriage and kids but when she said the name Players, he perked up.

"Eric Players", the woman pointed again at the house across the street. "He's our newest neighbor. He's the one that Miss Avery has been seeing. He probably knows where she is. She might even be there with him. I'd check it out if I were you. She won't come over here for coffee, but she sure has been spending a lot of time over there. Guess I'm not as interesting." And with that, Mrs. Chatterly closed the door.

Don didn't get a chance to thank the woman again; she didn't realize she had given him just the information he needed. He turned and hurried back to Julie's place to get his car. He decided on the walk down the hill to drive his car up and park in front of Eric Player's house before he rang the doorbell. He adjusted the strap of his holster under his jacket. He wanted to be ready. After the information he had found out about Eric Players and the construction accident, he wanted to be alert and prepared when he talked with him. And now that Mrs. Chatterly thinks Julie might be there, Don wanted to be ready for anything.

Eric didn't answer until after the third ring and Don had been ready to take a walk around the house when the door opened. "Yes?" Eric said. "Are you selling something? I'm not interested and I don't want any literature about your religion either. And no political campaign stuff." He began to shut the door.

"No, sir, I'm not selling anything or soliciting." Don responded. "Are you Eric Players?" Don asked him.

"Who wants to know?" Eric said.

Don realized this guy was sounding like trouble, so he extended his badge. "My name's Don Graverton, I'm a Detective with the Fort Wayne Police. Can we talk a moment Mr. Players?"

"Oh, sure. I'm sorry. I didn't mean to be rude." Eric's tone changed quickly. "It's just that we get so many solicitors here and with the campaigns starting up, you know, there are a lot more than usual this year. What can I help you with, Detective?"

"No problem, I understand, they can be a pain in the butt, huh? My wife complains about them all the time too." Don wanted to make Eric feel at ease so he would be receptive to questions. "May I come in?"

Eric didn't really want to let the detective in but he wasn't sure how to refuse without making the detective suspicious. "Sure, where are my manners, of course, come in."

Eric led the way to the kitchen. "Can I offer you a cup of coffee or tea? It won't take a minute." Eric offered in the hopes that this detective wasn't here about the construction accident. "What's a detective from Fort Wayne doing in Monique? It's a pretty quiet little town; that's why I moved here. I don't know what I can help you with; I don't go out much. I'm taking care of my invalid father, so I stay close to home most of the time."

Don followed Eric to the kitchen. "Coffee would be nice, thank you. I've been on the road all morning and haven't even had lunch yet. A cup of coffee would hit the spot if it's not too much trouble." Don figured the longer it took to get the coffee and drink it, the longer time he would have to visit with Eric Players.

Eric had a pot of coffee on the counter that had gotten cold, but he poured a cup and slipped it into the microwave. "So, Detective, uhhh, Graverton, did you say? How can I help? Has there been a robbery or something in the neighborhood? It's a pretty quiet place to live. I haven't heard anything. The neighbors have all been nice since me and my dad moved in even though I don't see them much. They even threw a welcoming BBQ. Real nice. Mrs. Chatterly across the street usually knows what's going on; have you talked to her?" Eric hoped his chit chat sounded casual enough.

"Yes, I did talk to her and well, actually she told me to come see you." Don said. "I'm inquiring about one of your other neighbors. A Miss Avery, Julie Avery. Do you know her?"

Eric tried to remain calm. "Oh, yeh, she's the writer who lives down at the end of the cul-de-sac. Really nice gal."

"Mrs. Chatterly across the road, said she thought you and Miss Avery were seeing each other." Don figured he might as well jump in since he was sure he had seen someone looking out the window while he was talking to Mrs. Chatterly.

"Yes, Julie is a great gal, but we're not *seeing* each other, at least not how you mean *seeing*. She helped me when we had that storm several weeks ago and then I helped her find a new car when hers got totaled in the parking lot at the mall. And we've had lunch and supper a couple of times. It's nothing serious, just friends getting together. We've been thanking each other, you know." Eric was worried he was rambling and it would make him seem nervous.

"Oh, how did she help you in the storm?" Don asked as he sipped his coffee hoping to keep Eric talking. He seemed to be spilling out information.

"Well, my dad is in a medically induced coma and on life support and when the power went out, I was concerned that the machines might shut down. Julie's house was the only one with lights on so, I went down there. She was kind enough to let me use her phone. Of course I found out later the machines have a backup battery that kicks in, dumb me." Eric was indeed spilling everything out too fast and he knew it. 'Calm down. Just give the facts. Let him ask the questions,' he told himself.

Don kept the conversation going by saying, "That was nice of her. Why was her house the only one with lights on if there was a storm that took everyone's out?"

"She has a backup generator she said. I guess writers are afraid to lose everything on their computers if the power goes out." Eric tried to laugh calmly.

Don knew he was getting this Eric guy to ramble. "So, it was after that you started dating? Good way to meet someone, in a thunderstorm." Don let out a little laugh.

"Well, we aren't really dating. I helped her when her car got wrecked and she fixed me lunch and we got to talking about our ability or inability to cook, so then I invited her over for Spaghetti Bolognese, my only good dish next to the chili I make on a cold day. You know, to thank her for helping me during the storm. After that she wanted to cook a roast and Yorkshire pudding to thank me for helping with the car. Crazy really, just going back and forth thanking each other." Eric just couldn't shut up. He knew he was talking too fast and too much. His nerves were getting the best of him.

"Yeh, that does sound crazy. I guess that's how romances start though." Don concluded.

"Oh, no, we aren't in a romance. We're just friends." Eric knew he was getting in too deep and wanted to get rid of the detective before he said anything else. "If you're through with your coffee Detective, I really have some things to do."

"Oh sure, I'm just about done. The reason I wanted to talk to you though, was because nobody has heard from Julie for a couple of days and when I was at her house a little while ago, she wasn't there, but I heard a cat meowing."

"On, no Spot is there by himself? That's not good. Maybe I should go get him. I cat sat once when Julie went to Fort Wayne overnight." Eric was actually concerned about Spot.

"Well, I don't think you can get in, I tried all the doors and the windows are locked down too. But that's nice of you to be concerned about the cat. I'm sure Julie would appreciate it." Don shared.

"It's what friends, do I guess. I hope Julie will be back soon. Will you let me know if you hear anything? I hope she's alright." Eric wanted his voice to sound sincere as he reached for Detective Graverton's coffee cup.

Don knew he was being excused, so he got up and headed for the door.

Julie was just down the hall and she had heard the guy when he came to the door and had listened to what she could hear of the bits of conversation that was going on with Eric and this guy who said he was a detective. 'Brandon's friend?' She wondered. 'If I can only get him to hear me.'

Julie tried to make some kind of noise, but the duct tape was too tight. She could only make a slight muffled groan. She knew no one could hear that. She struggled to get lose and couldn't budge the rope or the duct tape. Finally, with one surge of energy, she flung her bound up legs over and kicked at the night stand and the lamp there fell to the floor with a loud crash.

"What was that?" Don asked. Is there someone here?" He wanted to check the house further.

"It's my dad. I'd better go see if he's alright. Thanks for stopping Detective. Would you like me to call you if I see Julie come home? Do you have a card?"

Don realized he was being ushered out and there wasn't much else he could do but it raised his suspicions even more. "Yes, if you would, that would be wonderful, Mr. Players. Thank you for your time. Hope your dad is ok. Can I help in any way?" Don tried to stall his leaving in case he heard anything else.

Eric desperately wanted this detective out of his house immediately before Julie was discovered. "No, no, that's alright. I'm sure he is, he does move around a bit and sometimes he knocks things off the bed."

Don thought that was a strange thing to say about someone in a medically induce coma, but he had no further reason to stay, so he nodded and stepped out the front door. But he certainly was going to watch Mr. Players closer.

CHAPTER 13

Eric hurried down the hall and into the spare bedroom where Julie lay twisted on the bed. The lamp was on the floor and he knew she had been trying to signal that detective. "You awake again, my dear Julie. Why can't you be a good girl? It's a good thing I put that duct tape back. Even though you promised, I know you would have been screaming for help. I guess you will need a bigger dosage now. I can't trust you at all."

Julie wanted to scream, 'Oh, please Eric, don't drug me. I'm sorry. I won't do it again.' She knew he would never believe her no matter how hard she would plead.

"Funny that this happened when there's a detective here in the house. You were hoping he would hear you and come investigate. Who are you trying to kid?" Eric pulled the tape off her mouth and Julie desperately tried to explain hoping he would believe her.

"It was an accident, Eric, really. I was only trying to turn over. These ropes are too tight and they're hurting me. What detective? Why would a detective be here?" Julie hoped Eric would think she didn't know anything about Brandon's detective friend. She knew for sure now it was Don Graverton and he was investigating Eric and the construction accident just as he had promised Brandon. Maybe she could get Eric talking about it and he would forget about drugging her. 'Oh, why didn't Graverton come back? Where did he go?' Julie hoped he was calling the police department for backup and they would raid Eric's house. "Was he asking questions about your dad's accident? Isn't that strange after all this time?"

"No, actually, he was asking about you, my dear. Seems you have gone missing. I wonder what I'm supposed to do with you now? If a detective is looking for you, someone must really be concerned." Eric had that strange look coming into his eyes again, that look that scared Julie.

Julie knew it was Brandon who had sent his friend to find her, but she didn't want Eric to know that. "It was probably my publisher, Richard Beasley with Tetonkian Romantics. You know, I told you I had finished my new book. Richard is getting ready to send it to the presses and he probably had some last minute changes to discuss. He would be frantic to find me. You know how publishers are."

"No, I don't know how publishers are and I don't care who sent that detective. He doesn't need to be snooping around here. If he comes back, I'll take care of him."

Julie was terrified of what Eric might do. 'Oh, God, Brandon was right; I shouldn't have gotten involved with a total stranger even if he did seem like a nice guy. Stupid me, I just *had* to find out more about the construction accident. My curiosity has gotten me into trouble this time for sure just like Mom warned me.'

Eric tightened the ropes and made sure the duct tape was good and tight and then left the room. Julie was glad he hadn't given her another sedative. She hoped he had forgotten. She decided to remain quiet and maybe he wouldn't come back for a while. She definitely didn't want another shot. She didn't know how long she had been out before. She was losing track of time. Had she been there two days now? Brandon and Richard must be frantic, as well as Spot.

Detective Graverton could see Eric Players looking out the window through the living room curtains as he sat in his car looking back at the house. He had sat there for a while wondering what Eric might do after he left. He must have gone to check on his dad like he said, but then he had returned to the living room and peeked out. There wasn't much else he could do, so Don decided to leave and go back to the office and see if his FBI friends had found out anything more about Streeter Construction and Folder Architecture. He knew there was something going on with that guy. Things just didn't seem to add up and the guy was so nervous when Don was talking to him. He had spilled the coffee when he poured it and he kept rambling and clearing his throat when he talked. Don's detective experience told him that there was more to this guy than meets the eye.

He got to the edge of town and the more he thought about Julie, the more concerned he became that Eric Players had something to do with her being missing. 'Why would she leave her cat alone at the house for two days and why would she leave and not tell anyone, especially Brandon and Richard? It just didn't add up. That chatterbox neighbor said she had seen Julie coming and going from Eric's place. Maybe she was there. But why wouldn't she come to the kitchen and say hello?'

'I should have stayed at the house after I heard that crash. People in comas don't thrash around in bed.' The more he thought about it, Graverton knew he had to turn his car around and head back. He chose to park his car a couple of blocks away where it wouldn't be seen by Eric, and to take the back yards when he got closer. He could always explain that he was on a case if anyone saw him and asked why he was sneaking around the back yards. The closer he got to Players' block, the more he was convinced that Players knew more about Julie than he was saying.

Fortunately, the way the houses were built next to the wooded area, it made it easy for Graverton to slip behind them and stay close to the tree line. A walking trail ended a couple of houses up the road where it turned and headed through the edge of the woods and back up to the main road where it crossed to a playground and a community pool beyond. The neighborhood was in the suburbs and was private but still provided amenities for families who wanted to be away from the bustle of the main part of town. He could see why it had been the perfect place for Julie to write. Her cottage at the end of the cul-de-sac would give her the privacy she needed. And of course, it also gave Eric Players the perfect anonymity he wanted.

Graverton left the walking trail, being careful to stay behind the trees as he made his way to the Players house. He hoped Eric wouldn't be looking out his back windows. The yard behind the Players house wasn't very large and there were several trees and bushes and flower beds scattered throughout. Graverton wondered how Players had time to keep that up. It was meticulously groomed and Graverton decided Players must hire a gardener to keep it looking so good. Someone to question in the future, if need be. At any rate, Graverton was glad that the yard was full of places for him to creep along towards the back of the house. He got down on his knees at first and then later onto his belly like a commando in a war zone. He didn't want Players to see him and he hoped none of the neighbors would either. He didn't need anyone reporting a potential burglar. He wasn't worried that he could explain what he was doing crawling around the backyard, but it might tip off Eric that he was on to him.

Don could see Players in the kitchen so he kept close to the ground out of his sight line. There was a room at the end of the house looking over the densest part of the woods. Graverton felt this was probably where Players was keeping his dad. No one would be in that part of the woods or yard so it would be away from curious eyes. He crawled up to the window. He could see that the blind and curtains were pulled, but he was able to see through the edge of the blind and could just make out a figure on the bed. It wasn't a hospital bed like he expected to see if Player's dad was in a medically induced coma hooked up to machines.

It was quiet in the room and Graverton craned his ear close to try to hear anything. No hum of machines like he had heard when he was in the house earlier. Then he heard the door open, followed by Players' voice! "How we doing Miss Julie? Your friend, Detective Graverton, just left. He was full of BS but he won't find out anything here, but you should have been nice and quiet like I asked."

Julie tried to moan out a response. Graverton could hear the muffled sound and knew that she must be gagged. He figured she was tied up in that room and the crash he had heard earlier was her trying to get his attention. 'Oh, for crying out loud, Graverton, what kind of a detective are you that you didn't insist on going down the hall with the guy?' Don berated himself.

He could hear Eric talking. "So if I get you something to eat, will you be still while I feed you? I like to take good care of my invalid patients as long as they cooperate. Dad should have cooperated and he wouldn't be where he is right now. But what else could I do? He knew Streeter was responsible for the accident and covered it up. Dad covered for him and then I covered it up too to protect Dad. As it turned out, actually, everyone came out of it smelling like a rose. Streeter didn't want any investigation into the accident and Folder didn't want it either. George was worried he might lose his investors or his business, so getting me to sign off on the settlement was the easy way out. Everyone got what they wanted, I guess. Except me. I'm the guy they screwed out of a job and a career. Dad will just have to stay where he is until I decide what to do with him."

Eric was rambling on while Julie listened. "What am I supposed to do now? Why did you have to get involved, Julie? Why did I let *myself* get involved with you? Stupid of me to let a beautiful woman lead me astray from my plans. I could have lived here quietly in Monique and no one would have known. After a while I could have said Dad passed away in his sleep. Of course, that is what would have happened with a little help from me. But you had to be so pretty and sweet. Too bad you're a writer with so much curiosity."

Julie just laid there and listened and outside the window Detective Graverton listened too. It was all perfectly clear now. Everything Eric said matched up with what his FBI friend had told him. Streeter had been the cause of the accident and Ben Players had covered it up and Eric had helped him. Eric just hadn't planned on taking the full blame and losing his job. Obviously, he was now getting even with his dad.

Graverton knew they were going to jail for Involuntary Manslaughter and more when this all came out. He knew he had to act fast before Eric did anything else to Julie and his dad. Julie had been the innocent one who stumbled onto the whole thing because of her curiosity and right now he had to find a way to get her out of there safely. He ducked down and inched his way around the house. The sliding glass doors leading to the patio presented a problem. He could see Eric had gone back to the kitchen and was fixing the meal he had promised Julie. 'Well, I can just wait him out and when he goes down the hall to feed her, I'll try the side door in the garage. Often times people forget to lock those.'

Eric was humming to himself as he fixed some soup and a sandwich. He remembered how Julie had done the same that first time when he had helped her get her groceries home after her car was damaged. They had enjoyed that lunch together. They might have had a good relationship if it wasn't for his dad! 'Damn it, why did he do it? Stupid old man! Well, I can still fix that situation and then Julie will be free to be with me. I just have to get rid of that detective guy. I don't need him snooping around here anymore. If he comes back, I will take care of him.'

The soup was hot and the turkey and cheese sandwich was ready, so Eric headed down to Julie's room with the tray. Graverton saw Eric leave the kitchen and he hurried across the patio and around the corner to the garage's side door. He tried the knob and it opened! He was right, he'd learned over the years that people lock their front doors and the garage door itself, but forget about that side door. Often times there's junk stacked in the corner blocking it and they just don't think about it. Fortunately, Eric didn't have much in the garage and Graverton quietly slipped in. He entered the kitchen and he could hear Eric talking to Julie down the hall.

"Okay, here's an early supper. Sorry, we missed lunch, but I had to deal with that stupid detective. But, let's enjoy this. Remember when you fixed soup and sandwich for us? That was nice. Too bad things had to turn out so differently, Julie. I will make it all better soon, you will see. Now, if I take off the duct tape, you won't yell, right?"

Julie nodded. She had decided to cooperate while they ate and then maybe she would try screaming before he taped her mouth again. Surely someone, maybe the neighbor across the street would hear. She didn't know that Detective Graverton had come back and was in the house. Eric sat the tray down on the nightstand and slowly pulled the duct tape off her mouth. "I'm sorry I've had to do this Julie, but if you stay quiet I will leave it off."

"I'm sorry too, Eric, I never meant to get involved with you and your dad and the accident. I didn't want to upset you or do anything about it; I was just curious. You know I'm a writer and I just always have to have answers. You can tell me everything and I'll be satisfied and then I'll forget all about it and we can go on from there." Julie hoped she was lying convincingly. "If you undo my hands, I can feed myself. Really, I'm sorry and I promise I won't try to get away. That smells good and I am hungry. Let's just enjoy supper like we did before all this happened." She fully intended to get away if the opportunity presented itself but she had to convince Eric that everything would be alright and they would still be friends.

"Alright, Julie, I hope I can trust you this time." Eric released the duct tape from her hands and loosened the rope that anchored her to the bed. With the rope loosened she could sit up to eat. "Oh, thank you. This is much better. Let's eat; I'm starved!" Eric chuckled at her enthusiasm. "It's just soup and sandwich; you know I can't cook much and I didn't have time to make Spaghetti Bolognese."

Julie laughed. "Well, can I look forward to it again sometime?" She hoped she was gaining his confidence. "I still need to sample your famous chili."

"That's right!" Eric sat on the edge of the bed and placed the tray on his lap between them. Julie took a scoop of the soup; it was too hot to eat, so she looked up from the soup to take a bite of the sandwich and she saw Detective Graverton at the edge of the door with his finger to his mouth telling her to 'shhhh'. He had his gun out and Julie reacted by flipping the tray and dumping the hot soup into Eric's lap. Eric screamed, "Why did you do that?" just as Graverton rushed into the room shouting, "Down on the floor Players, you are under arrest for kidnapping."

In a second it was all over. He tossed Eric to floor and pointed his gun at him and said, "You move and I will shoot you without a moment's hesitation." He handcuffed Eric and used some of the duct tape that Eric had used on Julie to bind Eric's ankles. Eric just laid there. He knew it was over too and he would be going to prison. He began to sob quietly and he knew the lies and the secrets were done and part of him was glad; he wouldn't have to deal with it anymore. But he mostly was sad that he would no longer have a chance to get to know Julie better. He had really liked her in spite of everything.

"Are you alright?" Graverton asked Julie as he untied her and got the duct tape off her ankles. When he pulled the blanket off her lap and went to help her up, he saw that Julie's slacks and underpants were pulled down, "Oh God, Julie, did he rape you?" He quickly covered her up. "I'm so sorry I didn't get here sooner. Did that guy hurt you?"

"No, no, he just did that so I could urinate into the **Chux**. He didn't rape me. In fact, he was really sweet and kind most of the time. It was so weird."

"What? What a sicko." Graverton knew he had just got there in the nick of time.

"He didn't really hurt me, just humiliated me, of course. He wasn't thinking clearly." Julie didn't know why she was defending Eric, other than she had really liked him and now she felt sorry for what the future held for him.

Detective Graverton called for assistance and an ambulance. He insisted that Julie go to the hospital and get checked out, including a rape kit even though Julie told him it wasn't necessary. "It's standard procedure in cases like this, ok? Where's Players' dad?" Julie pointed down the hall and Graverton left Julie to go check on Mr. Players.

By the time the ambulance and the police units arrived, Julie had gone to the bathroom and washed her face and combed her hair. She didn't want to go to the hospital but Graverton said it was required and she should talk to the police there so they could fill out the proper report. Maybe they would allow the rape kit to be overlooked if she explained it all to them. But she did need to be checked over.

"Have you called Brandon?" Julie asked Detective Graverton. "Yes, he's on his way and I think Richard is coming too. I told them to meet us at the hospital."

Julie thought about how she was going to explain everything to Brandon and by the time she had climbed into the ambulance and got to the hospital, Brandon was there to meet her. 'He must have driven like a maniac from Fort Wayne!' Julie was so surprised to see him.

When he saw Julie getting out of the ambulance, he limped towards her on his crutches, "Julie, oh, my God, are you alright?" Brandon threw his arms around her, "I don't know what I would do if anything happened to you. God, Julie, I love you so much," as he kissed the top of her head. "I know you don't feel the same way, but I can't hold it back. I've loved you since we were in high school. Please be okay, Julie." The words he had been holding in for long, spilled out of him, and he held tight to her.

"Brandon, I'm fine. He didn't hurt me. Just my pride, I guess. I should have known sooner what he was up to." Julie suddenly realized that Brandon was on crutches with a cast on his ankle. "Oh my God, what happened to you?"

"Oh, stupid me, riding my bike across town at rush hour not paying attention to the traffic light, I reared ended a car. Dumb, huh?"

"What were you doing going across town at that time of day; you never do that?"

"I was meeting Don to go over the information about Eric and his dad and the accident, but none of that matters anymore. Oh, Julie, I love you so much and I was afraid I'd lost you. I never imagined that he could hurt you; I just thought you had fallen in love with him."

"No, of course not; he was just a friend and not a very good one as it turns out. Wait, what did you just say? You love me?"

"I'm sorry, Julie, I shouldn't have said that out loud. But, I've held it in for so many years and when I thought something bad had happened to you, I was beside myself with worry. And now that you're okay, I just blurted it out. Forget I said it and we can go on being friends, right?" Brandon was desperate to know that Julie wasn't mad at him.

"But, you said you loved me. I know we have been friends for a long time and we always say 'love ya' when we say Goodbye, but do you mean *love* love?"

"I'm sorry, Julie, please forgive me." Brandon was afraid she would break off their friendship now that he had confessed his feelings.

"Forgive you? Forgive you for what? Brandon, I love you too! I have ever since you kissed me prom night back in high school."

"Huh? But you came to school the next day and broke up with me. I thought you hated the kiss."

"I know, I pretended it meant nothing. The kiss was magical, but I couldn't tell you that. We were leaving for different colleges in two weeks and I was afraid to be in love with you and have you find someone else at college. I thought it would be best if we just broke up. I was afraid you would break my heart or I would break yours. Silly of me. I should have told you that. But then, we decided to just be friends. And we have been; these past sixteen years have been wonderful."

"Yes, they have been. But, when I changed to **Purdue** in our Junior year it was to be with you. We renewed our friendship and I was hoping it would develop into something more. But you seemed happier for us to remain in the friend zone. I thought that's where you wanted us to be and I was happy to stay there as long as I was with you. We are both so silly; we could have really been together all these years. We've missed out on so much. We were dumb to let it go on for so long without telling each other how we feel."

"Oh, Brandon, we haven't missed anything. We *have* been together. We've enjoyed so many lovely times together at movies, plays, and the beach cabin weekends. I wouldn't want to give any of that up. And it will be even better from now on." Julie wrapped her arms around Brandon's neck. "You are never going to lose me, my dear friend, no matter how hard you might try."

Brandon looked down into Julie's grey/blue eyes that sparkled with all the love she had for him. He kissed her gently and she kissed him back. "There will be more where that came from," he said. "I certainly hope so," Julie sighed. "I've been waiting a long time."

As Brandon and Julie stood there entwined in each other's arms, Detective Graverton came up to them. "So, I see you two have finally opened up about your feelings. What took you so long, Brandon?"

Brandon gave an embarrassed laugh as Julie said, "We know, we were foolish. I guess it took getting kidnapped to wake me up that this is the guy I should be with always."

"It's about time. It couldn't happen to a nicer couple." Don slapped Brandon on the back and shook his hand then turned to Julie and gave her a hug. "What will happen to Eric?" Julie asked. She still had a spark of a connection to him. He had been a friend before all the weird stuff began and she knew he was in really big trouble.

Detective Graverton said, "Well, I don't think you will need to worry about him in your lives again. He will be going away for a long time."

"What will happen to his dad?" Julie asked. "Will he ever come out of his coma?"

"Well, I'm not a doctor, but if Eric has been taking good care of him and as soon as all the sedation is out of his system, he might make a complete recovery. Of course, he will be in as much trouble as Eric over the accident. They both knew about Streeter's underhanded dealings and the faulty materials. Ben Players knew there could be problems with that building when it was finished. Thank God it didn't get done and had people living in those apartments when it collapsed." Graverton relayed the rest of the info he had uncovered.

Brandon and Julie just stood there listening and shook their heads. "It's crazy what some people will do for money." Brandon said. "What about Streeter and Folder Architecture?"

"Folder will be okay. They didn't know everything that Streeter was up to and since Eric admitted fault, they were released from any liability. But Streeter will be up on charges. The trouble started with him trying to get the building completed within an impossible deadline. Most of the workers I interviewed knew there were problems. They didn't really want to say much but a few of them came to Ben with their concerns and he just passed them off; told them to keep their mouths shut and get back to work.

Then Eric confronted his dad when the change orders started coming in and Ben again just waved Eric off telling him it was none of his business. That's where all the problems between them started. Eric knew his dad was into something he couldn't get out of. But he couldn't get his dad to let him in on the details.

Some of the workers said Eric came to the job site regularly and he and Ben got into some awful arguments. They said Eric knew there were serious consequences coming and he tried to tell his dad. The whole thing was a disaster just waiting to happen."

"I'm surprised some of the men didn't come forward after the building collapsed. "I suppose they didn't want to get involved in a lawsuit or a criminal case." Brandon suggested.

"Who knows what people are thinking and what they will do. Eric Players should have come forward immediately." Graverton said.

"I'm sure he didn't want his dad to be found at fault. He probably never dreamed the building would collapse and that he would end up being the one to take the blame." Julie said.

"Yes, if he had come clean at the beginning maybe the bulk of the blame would have been on Streeter and Ben might have spent some time in prison, but now Eric and his dad are up for Manslaughter because of the deaths. Not to mention Eric kidnapping you, Julie." Graverton added.

"I don't need to file charges. He didn't hurt me. He's got enough to deal with. I'm okay." Julie said, her usual forgiving self.

"You are most certainly going to file charges!" Brandon interrupted.

"Brandon, I'm alright. Eric will have plenty to answer for. Let's just forget about him."

"Well, all I can say is if he had hurt you, I would have killed him." Brandon stated. Julie and Graverton just looked at each other and smiled.

"Come on, Julie, you need to get checked out at the hospital and I need to file that report." Detective Graverton said.

CHAPTER 14

Richard Beasley came hurrying down the hospital hall. "Julie, thank God, you are alright. Brandon would not have survived if anything had happened to you." Richard saw Brandon's arm around Julie and she had laid her head on his shoulder. "So you finally told her? And she feels the same way I see."

"You knew too?" Brandon asked.

"Who didn't? Everyone except you two." Richard laughed.

"Why didn't you say something?" Brandon was embarrassed that his boss had known he was in love with Julie.

"I should have. I wanted to bat the two of you over the head many times and say 'wake up', but I figured you would find out on your own eventually. Sorry that it had to take Julie being kidnapped to shake you up, Brandon." Richard shook his head.

"I know, I'm stupid, but she knows now." "And so do you," Julie chimed in.

"What will happen to Players?" Richard asked. "Will he be arrested?"

"Oh, yes, he already has and he will stand trial for what he's done. I would imagine he will be lucky to get life instead of the death penalty. If he's found guilty of the accident where people were killed, we won't see him around anymore. Detective Graverton seemed certain about it," Brandon said.

"Actually, I think he needs some psychiatric care." Julie said. "He acted so weird after he kidnapped me, nothing like the friend I thought I knew. He would go into kind of a glazed trance. It was frightening at times, but then he could be kind and gentle. So I hope his lawyer petitions for some kind of psych evaluation."

"What about his dad? He was involved in the cover up too, wasn't he?" Richard had heard it on the news already of the kidnapping in Monique and something about a man who had been kept in a coma for months.

Detective Graverton heard the question as he joined them and answered, "Well, I would imagine he'll be charged too. But I would guess he might get a lighter indictment since he was injured in the accident too and then kept in the coma by his son. A good lawyer could work a deal for him. Who knows?" Detective Graverton shrugged his shoulders. "I feel kind of sorry for the guy, but I think he's just as guilty as his son."

"I feel bad for him too." Julie's soft heart kicked in. "I wish there was something we could do. I guess I could be a witness as to the coma part."

"Julie, you can't save the world. If they're guilty, then they should be punished." Richard added his two cents worth. "I'm just glad you are okay. What a mad man; he definitely needs to be locked in a psych ward."

"He was very confused and weird, but he didn't really hurt me other than the duct tape and rope. I was more scared and humiliated than anything. I just hope he gets the help he needs." Julie suddenly realized that Spot was still at the cottage. "Hey, has anyone checked on Spot? My poor baby was left alone for two days!"

"Not to worry. When Don told me he had heard a cat in the cottage when he was looking around, I gave him my key to go in. Boy, was he glad to see someone. His bowls were empty and he meowed and meowed till Don filled them. He chowed down immediately. Poor little guy. He might be mad at you for a while, leaving him alone." Brandon warned Julie.

"I'll have to give him some special loving tonight. He'll be fine in a couple of days, I'm sure. I just wish I had listened to him earlier. He tried to warn me from going to see Eric. I guess I'm not smarter than my cat. And I don't know why I didn't put the 2/22 thing together sooner. Some investigative reporter I would make, huh? Julie laughed.

"Hey, Julie," Richard said. "You'll be glad to know, the Board approved your new book after I finished my last edit. If you make those few changes we talked about, we can get it on the presses. But you will need to decide on the title. New book is all you've ever called it."

"I guess, that's how I've always thought of it. What's wrong with New Book? Or we could call it 'A Dark & Stormy Night'." Julie joked as it started to rain and everyone laughed.

"No, we should definitely stick with **New Book**. Anyway, I think I'm starting to like the sound of it." Richard assured them.

They all laughed again and Julie put her arm around Brandon's waist and helped him hobble out the hospital doors to his car.

"Come on, let's get you home and out of this rain. I think you need more of a rest than I do." Julie said as she hung onto him.

As they were crossing the parking lot, Richard called out, "Hey, everyone, it's 2:22 and I haven't had lunch yet. Anyone else hungry? Why don't we all go to Chamberlain's for a little celebration; my treat. The Players boys will be going to jail, everyone is safe, and Julie's new book is going on the presses. It's time to celebrate and I'm ready for some of their delicious Spaghetti Bolognese. Who's with me?"

Julie shuddered; not from the rainy weather OR the mention of Spaghetti Bolognese; but the thought of the number 222 again chilled her to the bone. Brandon hugged her close as they made their way across the parking lot, but she couldn't help thinking to herself, 'Now that Eric's going to jail and I have a bright future with Brandon, why does that number 222 frighten me?'

She tried to shake the thought that there was something not quite resolved.

The Julie Avery Mystery Trilogy.

THE CURSE OF APARTMENT 5B is Part 2
in this mystery trilogy.

Richard Beasley, Julie's publisher was pleased with HER NEW BOOK. It had sold well in the bookstores and online. He was anxious for Julie to continue providing her novels to him for publication, especially since she had added the mystery twist to HER NEW BOOK. Richard is equally pleased when Julie sells her cottage in Monique and moves to Fort Wayne. His and Brandon's offices are downtown, not far from Julie's new apartment. He is excited for the opportunity to work closer with Julie and to get her current book. He loves the story line she shares with him about the strange happenings at the West End Manor and the interesting people who live there. As we meet and get to know the residents, we find Julie's life is hectic as she plans for her upcoming wedding while researching the background of the curse of Apartment 5B for her current book. Watch for this Part 2 about author Julie Avery's life coming soon.

www.ingramcontent.com/pod-product-compliance
Lightning Source LLC
LaVergne TN
LVHW011935070526
838202LV00054B/4660